In the split second before I saw him, I'd thought I was imagining his voice. But Sean Kenley was very real. He stood on the other side of the front counter staring back at me with those incredible green eyes of his.

"Sean." When his name left my lips, it sounded far away.

Sean's dark hair was longer and even more tousled than normal. It sported the lighter streaks that usually didn't appear until midsummer. Those simple differences made me want to cry. I'd already accepted that I might never see him again, especially since we hadn't even been talking to each other when he'd left at the end of last year's rafting season.

Sean wasn't supposed to be here. He wasn't part of the Summer of Moving On.

HEARTBREAK RIVER

Tricia Mills

RAZORBILL

Heartbreak River

RAZORBILL

Published by the Penguin Group
Penguin Young Readers Group
345 Hudson Street, New York, New York 10014, U.S.A.
Penguin Group (USA) Inc., 375 Hudson Street, New York, New York 10014, U.S.A.
Penguin Group (Canada), 90 Eglinton Avenue East, Suite 700, Toronto, Ontario,
Canada M4P 2Y3 (a division of Pearson Penguin Canada Inc.)
Penguin Books Ltd, 80 Strand, London WC2R 0RL, England
Penguin Ireland, 25 St Stephen's Green, Dublin 2, Ireland
(a division of Penguin Books Ltd)
Penguin Group (Australia), 250 Camberwell Road, Camberwell, Victoria 3124,
Australia (a division of Pearson Australia Group Pty Ltd)
Penguin Books India Pvt Ltd, 11 Community Centre,
Panchsheel Park, New Delhi – 110 017, India
Penguin Group (NZ), 67 Apollo Drive, Mairangi Bay, Auckland 1311, New Zealand
(a division of Pearson New Zealand Ltd)
Penguin Books (South Africa) (Pty) Ltd, 24 Sturdee Avenue,
Rosebank, Johannesburg 2196, South Africa
Penguin Books Ltd, Registered Offices: 80 Strand, London WC2R 0RL, England

10 9 8 7 6 5 4 3 2 1

Library of Congress Cataloging-in-Publication Data
Mills, Tricia
Heartbreak River/by Tricia Mills
p. cm.
Summary: When her father dies when while whitewater-rafting, sixteen-year old Anna
feels responsible, but when tragedy strikes again she must face her deepest fears in
order to reclaim her love of the Colorado river where she grew up--and of the boy she
grew up with.
ISBN 978-1-59514-256-6 (paperback)
1. River life--Colorado--Fiction 2. Rafting (Sports) --Fiction 3. Death--Fiction 4. Guilt-
-Fiction 5. Interpersonal Relations--Fiction 6. Colorado--Fiction
PZ7.M63987 He 2009
[Fic] 22
2008021062
Printed in the United States of America

HEARTBREAK RIVER

CHAPTER 1

I pressed the phone closer to my ear, trying to hear my grandfather's request over the noise of a half dozen motor-cycles roaring up Cooley Mountain Road. I watched through the office's screen door as the helmetless riders met the beginning of another Colorado summer, and quite possibly some bugs, head-on.

"Bring me some of those gummi fish. Those things are addictive," Grandpa Bert said low. I pictured him looking over his shoulder to make sure he wasn't overheard.

I glanced toward the snack displays on the opposite side of the large, open cabin that served as the home of Cooley Mountain Whitewater Rafting. I felt a bit like my grandpa's drug dealer. Only his drug of choice was candy.

Just call me Alex Landon, sugar pusher.

"You know Grandma doesn't want you eating so much sugar. She'll filet me if she catches me."

"Oh, come on, feel sorry for your poor grandpa. I've got a broken leg, you know."

He sounded so pitiful, milking his recent fall for all it

was worth, that I couldn't help laughing. "Okay, I'll smuggle some home after work today," I said, then hung up.

The warmth of early summer wafted through the screen, just as it had the previous sixteen summers of my life. If I hadn't known this would be my last season at Cooley Mountain, I'd have made a mad push for air-conditioning.

I mean, seriously, my legs made that oh-so-attractive unsticking sound as I lifted myself out of the faux-leather desk chair. On the way to retrieve Grandpa's gummi fish before anyone else showed up, I switched the ceiling fan up another notch.

I grabbed the top bag of gummis from the wooden shelves, made a note of their price on my charge list, and slipped them into my purse in the bottom desk drawer. I chuckled as I imagined my face on a Wanted poster for sugar trafficking.

"She seemed like such a nice girl," the neighbors would say as the police cuffed me and dragged me away from my life of sweet, sweet crime.

Almost simultaneously the back and front doors burst open. Through the front entered a family of tourists. Streaming through the back door into the log building were several of my always-joking-around male coworkers. Tommy Lewis, our temporary resident Brit. Chad Bingham, built like a linebacker with a buzz cut because he was one on the Golden Bend High School Cougars team. Daniel Weatherly, smart, always reading, and quiet most of the time. But when he did talk, there was no mistaking he wasn't a native. All he had to do was open his mouth and Southern rolled out.

"Excuse me," the tourist dad said as he stepped up to the front counter. Even before I reached the family, I had them pegged as clueless, thanks to their rapid-fire questions.

"How many bathrooms are there along the route?"

"Will we get very wet?"

"Can I take my PSP?"

I stared at the family on the other side of the front counter from me. Yet again I was amazed by the complete ignorance of some of the tourists who found their way through the front door of our family's business. Another aspect I wouldn't miss.

"There aren't any bathrooms. It's a wild river, with no facilities of any kind. On the daylong trips, there are two scheduled stops, one at lunch, one midafternoon. And there are plenty of large boulders to provide cover."

It took a Herculean effort not to snort when I saw the mom's face contort into the universal expression for "Eew!"

"As for getting wet," I said as I turned to Mr. I Must Work in Something Terribly Exciting, Like Insurance, "yes, you'll get soaked." The framed photos of previous rafting expeditions lining the walls might have offered a smidge of a clue.

I didn't even answer the boy's PSP question. It was just too stupid for words.

"Carl, this isn't for us," the woman said as she placed a brochure about the rafting trip options back on the counter. "I came on vacation to relax. This is not relaxing."

Without waiting for a response, she turned and strode toward the door, no doubt about to direct her husband to the nearest hotel with a pool and quite possibly an expensive spa.

Though our family's livelihood depended on tourists actually taking raft trips down the Grayton River, I was glad to see these people vacate the premises. The last thing we needed was a bunch of rafters thinking this was going to be a Disneyland ride.

"Morons, the lot of them," Tommy Lewis said in my ear. The way he said it in his British accent made me laugh, as if the startling increase in idiots in America were lamentable.

I moved toward the desk, where a stack of paperwork awaited my attention. "Honestly, they should have to wear T-shirts or something to label themselves."

Tommy, who was in month six of his year with his aunt here in Colorado to get "the American experience," leaned back against the counter in his casual way, Mr. Supreme Self Confidence. "Now, fair Alex, that would ruin the fun of trying to pick them out before they open their mouths."

"True." I retrieved a ponytail holder from a desk drawer and wrestled my shoulder-length, wavy, contrary dark hair into a ponytail, then fanned my sweaty neck. "What is up with the temperatures? It's not supposed to be this warm for another month."

Daniel snorted as he walked past the desk holding a bottle of water. "You think this is hot? It's only eighty degrees outside."

"Yes, I know you come from Roastville, Tennessee, but here it's hot for early June."

To his credit, Daniel didn't launch into how lucky we were in the lack-of-humidity department.

Tommy pushed away from the counter and plopped

down on the end of my desk, making the wood squeak. "You need your own personal cooling device," he said, then blew air toward my exposed neck.

I swatted him on the arm, making him and the other guys laugh. "I'm fairly certain you all have things to do other than bug me." I made a shooing motion toward all of them.

Tommy uttered a dramatic sigh as he slid off the desk and ambled to the counter to consult the day's schedule. "Too bad you ran off the Clueless Wonders. I could have had fun with them out on a trip."

My hand clenched the pen I was using to pay the electric bill. Tommy was a fun guy to hang out with, and I could have listened to him read the IRS code all day and found it fascinating, but he possessed a daredevil streak that made me nervous.

"No hotdogging on the river. We don't want anyone getting hurt."

Or worse.

I focused on the strong, bright sunshine bathing the mountains outside. A powerful, positive image to match the upcoming summer months. I wanted to walk out into those rays and let the warmth soak into me despite how flushed I already felt, let the heat burn away any negative thoughts or sad memories.

Tommy retraced his steps, bumped the end of my nose lightly with the knuckle of his forefinger, and smiled at me. "You worry way too much, love." He leaned forward.

Okay, so most girls wouldn't have minded tall, blond, and tanned Tommy Lewis with his intoxicating accent striding into their personal space and taking up residence, but I didn't have the experience necessary to deal with said British invasion.

I'd worked here, surrounded by good-looking teenage river rats, for years. But for most of that time I was just one of the guys. I had eventually begun to develop physically, to actually look like a girl with—gasp!—breasts. When the guys began to take notice was when my dad laid down the law, making it clear that the boss's daughter was off-limits. I was a coworker, nothing more.

Yeah, my social life was smoking hot after that.

But now Dad was no longer here to keep guys like Tommy at bay.

"Quit flirting with her, Tommy," Chad said as he punched Tommy playfully in the shoulder. "It won't do you any good. You still have to work as much as the rest of us."

Chad should have known. He'd tried the flirting route once upon a time, and it had earned him nothing but a glass of ice water over his head. That's how Dad had dealt with my hormonal coworkers. Everyone except Sean.

I stood so quickly I banged my knee against the underside of the desk and uttered a curse that would have made my grandma's bobbed gray hair stand on end. At least the throbbing was something to focus on other than Sean Kenley. I'd be glad when I got to the point when I didn't have to keep reminding myself that Sean belonged to the past, and that I was living only for the now and the future from this point forward.

"But she's just so darn cute, it's hard to resist," Tommy

said. "Plus, I had to do my manly duty and protect her from a pack of wild dumb-asses."

Feeling like a blooming idiot for cracking my knee and for leaping to my feet for no discernable reason, I decided to play along with Tommy.

"Lordy, yes, I don't know what I would've done without you, kind sir," I said as I placed the back of my hand to my forehead and feigned a truly bad Scarlett O'Hara accent.

Daniel rolled his eyes. "We do not sound like that."

The rest of us burst out laughing because he did indeed sound like he'd stepped out of *Gone with the Wind*.

"Y'all suck," Daniel said, which only made the rest of us laugh harder.

"Sounds like I'm missing all the fun."

My head whipped around so fast I made myself dizzy. In the split second before I saw him, I'd thought I was imagining his voice, was hoping I had. But Sean Kenley was very real. He stood on the other side of the front counter staring back at me with those incredible green eyes of his.

"Sean." When his name left my lips, it sounded far away, as if my ears were stuffed with cotton.

"Hey." He broke eye contact, and my chest felt like it was being pressed by a vice.

"Dude!" Chad said. "Didn't expect to see you."

I was only half aware of Chad glancing my direction. Too stunned to know what I should say next, I kept staring. Sean's dark hair was longer and even more tousled than normal. It sported the lighter streaks that normally didn't appear until midsummer. Those simple differences made me want to cry.

I hadn't seen him for nine months. Nine horrible, lonely, dark months. I'd already accepted that I might never see him again, especially since we hadn't even been talking to each other when he'd left at the end of last year's rafting season.

Sean wasn't supposed to be here. He wasn't part of the Summer of Moving Forward plan.

Could the guys see the fog surrounding me, only allowing part of their conversation to penetrate? I caught snatches about mountain climbing and the skiing he'd done over the winter. That explained the newly defined muscles in his tanned arms, the sun-bleached blond intermingling with his darker hair. I wondered what else I'd missed while he'd spent the school year in Denver with his mother after his parents' divorce.

Chad and Daniel introduced him to Tommy. When Tommy's eyes met mine, his held a question. It was enough to snap me out of my daze.

"Why are you here?" I asked.

Sean barely looked at me. "To work for the summer, like always."

Like always. It couldn't be *like always*. My heart beat faster and faster, and I fought the need to sink into the chair. Why had he come back, when he could have gotten a job so many other places? I dissected his every word, every movement. We've been friends all our lives, but that was before I screwed up everything. Was he thinking of my idiocy when he gave me cool, expressionless answers and averted his eyes?

Or maybe he was just feeling out the situation, seeing

how I'd react to him. But what if that distance was a product of him being totally over me? Was that why he had nothing to say?

"Oh," I finally said. My brain refused to produce anything else for my mouth to utter.

"I talked to your grandfather."

I thought of the gummi fish and imagined slamming them back onto their display in protest. Why had Grandpa Bert brought Sean back this summer? He knew we had broken up, even if he wasn't privy to all the details. Betrayal crept up my throat and threatened to choke me.

I noticed a couple of quick glances from the guys my direction. I wouldn't have them feel sorry for me, to think me weak.

"Don't you all have work to do?"

"All done, boss," Tommy said. "Just waiting for the rafters."

I hated being called the boss, but that's exactly what I was. I might have only been sixteen going on seventeen, but I helped my grandparents run a business while planning for my senior year of high school and counting down the days until I could leave Golden Bend and Cooley Mountain Rafting behind. A year ago, I couldn't have even imagined leaving.

But a lot could happen in a year.

I fought my flight response for several more minutes, forced myself to listen to the guys chatting as if nothing out of the ordinary was happening. I waited until Tommy headed for the restroom and Sean stuck his head in the fridge in the corner before I slipped out the back door. I made my way down the hill to the rafts loaded and ready to be pushed into the river.

The soaring height of Cooley Mountain with its green cloak of lodgepole pine reflected in the wide expanse of the Grayton River. The water ran deceptively calm along this stretch. Someone unfamiliar with the river's personality would never guess that only a couple of miles downstream, it narrowed as it surged through a series of red rock canyons. The Grayton boasted some of the best class 4 and 5 rapids in the world. Beautiful. Challenging. Deadly.

I shook my head, as if I could erase the memories like a crudely drawn picture on an Etch-A-Sketch. Sean was here, but I could still look forward. Pretend nothing had ever happened. That would certainly prove easier than acknowledging that Sean probably didn't want anything to do with me anymore.

Two minivans full of today's customers pulled into the parking lot at the top of the hill, so I made quick but careful work of checking all the ropes tying down the supplies and safety gear. I tested every last knot to make sure they were tied securely and ran through a mental checklist of the safety gear.

"Did the new guy tie the knots?"

I gasped and spun to see Sean standing there, a cold Coke in his hand.

"What?"

He nodded toward the raft. "I figure you must be checking

Tommy's work, because everyone else has been doing this since we were fourteen."

I looked over at the raft and wiped my hands on the front of my khaki shorts, unable to admit I had no idea who'd tied the gear down. "Can't be too careful."

When I glanced at him, I saw the shared memory reflected in his eyes and had to look away again. Though the sound of the rapids wasn't audible from here, the river seemed to roar in my ears. Sweat trickled down my neck as I wondered what was going through Sean's head. Was he thinking up a way to tell me what a bitch I'd been when we'd last seen each other?

I closed my eyes and forced my breathing to slow. I inhaled a deep breath, smelled sun-warmed earth and pine, the dampness of the riverbank.

If Sean had planned to say something else, he lost his chance when Tommy, Chad, and Daniel showed up at the launch point with the day's rafters. For the next few minutes, we ushered everyone into the three rafts, gave them their life vests and last-minute safety instructions, and went over the overnight trip's itinerary one more time. All the while, Tommy the court jester kept everyone entertained.

"And there's an old river-running tradition that guarantees good luck and fun for all," he said as he stepped toward me.

Before I could imagine what he was up to, he grabbed my face and planted a kiss on my lips. I stood there with everyone staring at me, struck dumb by what had just happened.

"If you kiss the boss lady before you leave, it's massive good luck," Tommy said as he hopped into his raft, grinning wide.

My brain finally reengaged and embarrassment heated my face as the guys pushed off into the river, Sean usurping Daniel's spot in one raft at the last moment. Though I couldn't look at Daniel beside me or meet Tommy's eye, I did notice the expression on Sean's face. He wasn't looking at me or at Tommy, but the tightness of his jaw certainly didn't make him appear happy.

Was he upset because he hadn't taken the chance to tell me how unfair I'd been to him last summer? Or was it the fact that I hadn't initiated an apology?

Daniel returned to the office as I watched Sean's profile moving farther toward the center of the river. The craziest possibility popped into my head. Could he be angry about Tommy's kiss because he still cared about me? Was I a fool, a glutton for punishment for even allowing myself to wonder? No matter—the idea took root. An excitement that I hadn't felt in ages surged through me. When the rafts disappeared around the bend below the put-in point, I started running. Spruce and cottonwood limbs slapped me in the face as I headed up another hill, but I batted the attacking branches out of my way. I finally reached the edge of the rocky overhang above the river.

Tommy Lewis had just kissed me, but Sean was the one I watched as his strong arms flexed with each stroke of the oars. Inside me, I felt something awaken, something I hadn't thought I'd ever feel again.

Hope.

CHAPTER 2

After I returned to the office, I answered e-mail, updated our Web site, booked a church group rafting trip for July, and stocked the shelves with the latest delivery of trail mix, chips, and drinks. Those tasks finished, I was left staring at the wall and replaying the morning's events in my head. I thought about Tommy's kiss. It'd been all warm and salty, nothing like Sean's slower kisses that had often tasted of the sour apple Jolly Ranchers he constantly popped in his mouth.

I leaned back and redirected my stare to the ceiling beams, at the oars, life vests, and inflated raft that hung from the rafters as part of the rustic decor. Of course, "rustic" didn't mean "dirty", and I couldn't remember the last time those things had been dusted. I closed my eyes and tried to convince myself I wasn't crazy in thinking Sean might still care about me, at least a little.

For years I'd pined away for Sean, at first too scared to say anything to him about it, and then prevented by my dad from doing anything more than thinking about the guys I worked with. But then one day last summer everything had changed.

I stood and walked around the cabin, straightening items that didn't need straightening, trying to forget. It was safer to forget how I still felt about Sean deep inside than risk believing we could start over, wasn't it?

But what if I had seen the jealousy I'd thought I saw earlier? What if we were both waiting for the other to make the first move toward reconciliation?

I pressed the base of my palm against my forehead, trying to alleviate the headache building there. Why was I driving myself crazy? It wasn't like I could tell Sean how I felt now anyway. He was miles downriver and wouldn't be back until tomorrow.

But what about tomorrow?

Thankfully, the phone rang, giving me a reprieve from the yo-yoing of my brain.

"Cooley Mountain Whitewater," I answered, megathankful for the distraction.

While I scheduled another group trip, the screen door opened.

"Girl, we have got to talk."

I glanced over at Mala, my best friend and cousin, and pointed toward the phone I was obviously using. Mala just crossed her arms over her ample breasts, lifted an eyebrow toward her crown of long, blonde hair, and gave me one of her "any day now" looks.

I rolled my eyes and finished the booking before hanging up.

"About time," Mala said as she walked around the end of

the counter, revealing that she was wearing white shorts and a scoop-neck Cooley Mountain tank.

"Hello, working here," I said as I glanced at the clock on the wall. "Which you were scheduled to be doing fifteen minutes ago."

"Nag, nag, nag. I was busy getting the scoop that I *should* have been getting from you."

Crap, she knew about Sean. I so wasn't ready to talk about this.

"Tommy Lewis kisses you and you don't immediately call me? What's up with that?"

I scrunched up my forehead. "How in the world do you know about that?"

"So it's true then?" Her voice rose an octave at the indignity of not being the first stop on the gossip train.

"Yes, shockingly enough. Now how do you know?"

She paced in front of my desk, using her hands to help her talk. Mala was one of those people who probably couldn't speak if someone tied her hands behind her back. "I was at the coffee shop, and I overheard Eric Schulman talking to some of the other mental giants of Golden Bend. Evidently, Tommy called him from the river to share the news."

Tommy called Eric? Man, I hated male bragging rituals.

"Tommy was just being his normal self, showing off for the tourists. You know how he is."

Mala directed her bright blue gaze at me. "Laying a big, wet one on his boss seems a bit extreme, even for him."

"It wasn't that big of a kiss, and it definitely wasn't wet! Just a smack and run really. Commonly known fact: Guys *exaggerate*."

"You *do* know that every girl in school is going to hate you now, right?"

"Does that include you?"

"Me?" Mala shrieked this as if I'd accused her of high treason. "Not hardly. I'm not going for a guy who flirts with everything that has boobs. No offense."

"I find that hard to believe," I said and made a vague gesture toward the words *Cooley Mountain* stretched across her chest.

Her mouth dropped open in such dramatic fashion that I couldn't help a snort of laughter.

She flopped down onto the worn love seat against the wall, looking out of place against the frayed taupe fabric that was as old as she was. "So what was it like?"

"What?"

Mala rolled her eyes. "I know you're not that thick."

"Really, it was nothing. I mean, it surprised me more than anything. Even with him being such a ginormous flirt, I didn't see it coming."

"So no sparks?"

I let out a sigh. Mala had been trying to get me to date again for months, and it annoyed her to no end that I kept saying no. How could I enjoy myself on a date when my heart still belonged to someone else?

"No sparks."

"Well, there don't really have to be sparks at the beginning."

"Mala."

She gave a gesture of surrender. "Fine, fine. So, how did everyone react to the impromptu kissage?"

"The guests laughed and clapped, probably figured it was part of the trip package."

Mala propped her elbow against the arm of the love seat, leaned her jaw against her upturned palm. "What about the rest of the guys? Bet they had a good howl."

I shrugged. "I wasn't really paying attention." Because all my focus had been on Sean.

"Tommy's kiss stunned you that much, huh?" She waggled her eyebrows and gave me a wicked smile. "I think you might be lying about the lack of sparks."

"There were no sparks, okay?"

"Jeez, is snappish the new friendly?"

I wasn't sure why I didn't share more with her. Maybe because I feared I was imagining what Sean's reaction might have meant or that she'd think I was pathetic. She knew how long I'd liked Sean, how I'd messed up, how I was too embarrassed to call him to apologize. How over the winter I'd wanted desperately to stop liking him because I didn't want to feel anything anymore.

"It's been nine months, Alex. You could have had a freakin' kid in that amount of time."

"I'm well aware of how long it's been."

"You broke up with him, he left, it's over," she said,

accurately sensing where my thoughts had gone. She stood and strode past me toward the gift shop side of the room, probably headed for the fridge and a cold bottle of water. "You need to move on."

I hated it when Mala's bossy side came out, which it had more and more since my breakup with Sean. By virtue of being an entire three months older than me, she felt entitled to give random advice, even when I didn't want it. I wanted to shock her, to say something totally unexpected. "He's back."

She stopped and turned toward me. "What?"

Total disbelief showed on her face, but it didn't give me the satisfaction I'd hoped it would. It just opened up the door to talking about Sean, and how I'd ruined the best thing that ever happened to me. I lowered my eyes to the scuffed hardwood floor.

"Sean's back for the summer."

"Don't tell me he's working here."

"He's working here."

Mala braced her hand against the end of the countertop. "Did you call him?"

I could tell by the tone of her voice that it wasn't the supposed call that would upset her but rather me not telling her about it.

I shook my head. "Grandpa hired him back. I don't know who called whom."

Mala cursed before stalking the rest of the way to the refrigerator. She snatched a bottled water, twisted off the cap, and took a long drink before marching back toward me.

"Well, just because he's here doesn't mean you should go crawling back to him."

"I'm not crawling anywhere," I said, raising my voice. "Cripes."

Mala resumed her spot on the love seat. "Okay, I'm sorry. That was harsh. I just know how this whole mess has affected you."

"It could be different this time. I think he might have been jealous when Tommy kissed me earlier." I allowed the voicing of my thoughts to fuel my hope. What if this could still be a summer of moving forward, but moving forward with Sean at my side?

Mala gave me a pitying look. "Please don't go down that road."

"Why not? Our breakup was my fault. I could make it right." I fought the desperation clawing at me.

Mala clasped her hands together. "I didn't want to have to tell you this, but I heard Sean's seeing someone."

My heart cramped. "How could you know that?"

"Daniel saw him in Denver, a couple of months ago. He was with some Barbie-looking girl."

That description was funny coming from Mala, who had a few Barbie-esque attributes of her own.

"Where did he see them?" Did I really want to know?

"At some big bookstore. Shocking, I know, Daniel in a bookstore." She nodded toward the sound of thumping outside, the sound of Daniel getting the gear ready for an hour-long trip I'd booked an hour ago.

"They could have been studying."

"Anatomy, maybe."

Should I ask Sean about this mystery girl, or should I take Mala's advice for once and simply get on with my Sean-less life?

Mala scooted to the edge of the love seat. "He's moved on. You should do likewise. You deserve to have some fun this summer. With Tommy, with Chad, with some random hot guy you see on the street."

I picked up a pencil and spun it on its tip atop the desk calendar. "I think I'll skip the picking up guys on the street. That's more up your alley."

"Ouch."

I somehow managed to laugh at her mock affrontedness. Mala was getting really good at making it look real. But she knew full well that there was some truth to my words. The girl had never had a long-term boyfriend, preferring to keep her options open.

"Can I help it if I live life to the fullest?" she asked. "I like to have fun. Where's the harm in that?"

She had a point. This would likely be my last summer at Cooley Mountain Whitewater. Having fun with my friends sounded really good right now.

Perhaps the miraculous would happen and, despite Mala's revelation, I'd even get up the nerve to tell Sean how I still felt about him. And he'd feel the same for me.

CHAPTER 3

As thunder rumbled over the mountains during dinner, I itched to drive back up to the office and radio Sean, to make sure he and the rest of the crew and guests were okay. Grandpa Bert caught my eye.

"No sense even trying," he said, reading my mind as well as Dad used to. "You know you won't be able to reach them down in that canyon."

I pushed away the lingering annoyance that Grandpa hadn't consulted me about Sean before hiring him back for the summer, hadn't even mentioned that he was returning. I'd thought of a million ways to confront him about the situation, but by the time I got home none had seemed worth it. My grandparents had gone through enough in the past year without me adding to their troubles. Plus, I'd never been able to stay mad at Grandpa. He had that effect on people. I'd even delivered the gummis as promised.

He was right about the canyon, of course. The overnight camping spot was on a sandy area in the heart of Blackbird Canyon, home to no communication with the outside world. Even though I knew all this, and even though I knew that despite their antics the guys were good river guides, I couldn't stop worrying. I hated being helpless, loathed it. Just to feel useful, I thought about calling up the U.S. Weather Service in Denver and asking, "What's the deal? How does a twenty percent chance of rain turn into ninety percent in eight hours' time?"

Instead, I cleared the plates from the table, scraped the crumbs into the trash, and loaded the dishes into the dishwasher that had only been added to the 1920s ranch house in the last year. Prior to that, Grandma had insisted she didn't mind washing the dishes by hand. Grandpa had finally stopped asking and just had it installed while Grandma was in Pueblo visiting Great-Aunt Jane. Of course, now Grandma was half in love with the dishwasher.

A clap of thunder and a flash of bright white lightning made me jump.

Nearly at the same moment, the phone rang. I walked across the room's yellow and white linoleum floor and lifted the receiver. I hoped the lightning didn't decide to run through the phone line and fry me up like bacon.

"Hello?"

"Alexandra?"

"Mom?" Who else? No one called me Alexandra but Mom. She did it in some long-held hope that I would suddenly become more feminine and want to go shopping for pink lace camisoles and frothy dresses. Hey, I liked cute clothes as much as the next girl, but I tended toward sporty and cute, not frilly and "cute."

"Yes, what's wrong with the connection?" she asked over the crackling in the phone line.

"We're having storms."

"Oh, I won't keep you long, then. How are you?"

"Fine. We're just finishing dinner."

"Grandma sent an e-mail, said Grandpa broke his leg."

I eyed Grandpa. "Yeah, he was pretending he was a twenty-year-old and took a less than graceful fall off the kayak storage rack."

"Just wait until I get this cast off, missy," Grandpa said as he shook his index finger at me.

I laughed, and so did Mom. It wasn't a sound I'd heard much in the past year.

First she'd had to deal with the changes in Dad after he came back from serving in the Middle East last May. Then his drowning three months later. Tears pooled in my eyes, and I looked at the ceiling to close off my tear ducts.

Mom hadn't been the same person since the river claimed Dad, since the rescue teams found his broken body far down river from what was supposed to be his takeout point. The familiar stab of pain hit me square in the chest, and I had to pause in my thoughts until it lessened.

Dad's death had been beyond horrible for everyone, but it had cracked something inside Mom.

My grandparents, worried about Mom's fragile state of mind, sent her off to Florida a month ago for some time away. Time away from responsibilities and everything that reminded her of Dad. Away from the fact that he wasn't here anymore and he was never coming back. She took walks on the beach and got massages at a spa. She was meeting with a therapist, though she didn't talk about that.

"So how's the beach?"

"Nice." She hesitated. "I'm beginning to feel better."

"That's good," I said past the annoying lump in my throat. "I'm glad."

Another boom of thunder and crack of lightning made me jump, followed by increased static on the phone line. My thoughts went back to Sean and the others. My stomach knotted at the thought of—no. Chad had been rafting for years. Tommy had run rivers all over the world. And Sean was an excellent rafter and guide.

But so was Dad.

My insides twisted some more, images of Dad mixing with those of Sean, Tommy, Chad, and the guests. I needed to get away from Mom and the memories talking to her dredged up. "Here, I'll let you talk to Grandma." When I handed over the receiver, I headed for the stairs. "I'm going to go check my e-mail. See you in the morning."

"Good night, dear," Grandma said, then placed a kiss on my cheek.

When I reached my room, however, I didn't turn on my computer. Instead, I opened the window and let the damp air flow over me. I lay down on the bed on my side, wrapped a pillow in my arms, and listened to the rain. And prayed that Sean and everyone else was okay down in that canyon.

● ● ●

The wind howled through the canyon, sounding like a wounded, angry animal intent on taking out its pain on others. The river churned, the water black with jagged whitecaps. Empty rafts floated by, followed by scattered cargo and ropes trailing through the waves, the knots untied.

My heart squeezed so hard I cried out, but my anguish was swallowed by the wind. Why hadn't I retied the knots tighter myself? Why hadn't I known the weather was going to turn dangerous?

Two oars flew by on the current, followed by a bashed Styrofoam cooler. A hat and a shoe tried to catch them.

Fat, scorching tears joined the raindrops coursing down my cheeks. "I'm so sorry."

I jerked awake and straightened up in bed, afraid I was having a heart attack.

"Shh, it's okay," Grandma said as she pulled me into her arms and gently rocked me like she probably had when I was a baby.

My pulse slammed so hard against my eardrums that for several seconds I couldn't even hear the rain that still pounded against the roof.

"I'm sorry I woke you," I said against Grandma's chest. She smelled like fresh laundry and a hint of the vanilla lotion she used.

Grandma ran her hand over my messy hair. "It's all right. I understand."

And she did. Even though she'd lost her own son, Grandma Grace had always been there for me after all my nightmares in the weeks following Dad's death. She was there to hold and comfort me when Mom was too fractured to do much more than breathe.

Grandma and I—we were cut deep as well, but we were Landon women, strong women whose heritage in the sometimes unforgiving mountains went back to before Colorado was a state. There had been lots of times in the past year when I felt more like cracking to pieces than being strong. But something I couldn't explain—maybe it was genes, after all—had kept me going even when I didn't think it was possible.

"It's been a while since you had one of your dreams," she said.

"It wasn't about Dad this time."

"The boys?"

"Yeah."

Why had I dreamed about them? Were Sean and the others really in danger tonight? Had I missed something important when I'd checked the rafts? The what-ifs assaulted me like they had in the days after Dad drowned. What if I hadn't gone with Sean instead of staying at work with Dad? What if I'd tried harder to reach Dad when he came back from his National Guard duty, to break through his shell?

"I know seeing Sean again today was likely hard, but Grandpa and I thought it best not to tell you. We hoped that seeing each other again after all these months would help you two get over whatever happened between you."

I knew they meant well, but I still wasn't sure how I felt about the situation. Part of me wanted so desperately to look at Sean's reappearance in my life as a chance to start over, but Mala's words about him having moved on with someone else kept coming back to me, haunting me.

Could I blame him? Did I expect him to wait around forever, especially after what I'd done? Still, it hurt that he could hook up with some other girl so easily when I couldn't carve him out of my heart.

I pulled out of Grandma's arms and kissed her cheek, one weathered by a lifetime of running the river. "Go on back to bed. I'll be fine."

She placed her cool hands on my cheeks, looked at me and nodded. "You will be. And so will the boys. Gut feeling."

We'd all learned to trust Grandma's gut feelings. They were almost always right.

Almost.

I glanced at the clock as Grandma left the room— 4:32 a.m. I walked to the window and stared out into the darkness, hoping Grandma's instinct was right this time and the river hadn't claimed another victim.

I sat on the floor next to the window and inhaled the scent of the rain. I even smiled when I thought about how cranky the guys would be when they arrived at the takeout point, most likely wet and chilled to the bone. But safe.

I had to believe that.

CHAPTER 4

The morning crawled at the pace of honey being poured at the South Pole. Granted, it was barely ten o'clock, and the rafters were only an hour late, but my nerves were stretched so taut that I literally couldn't sit still. I paced until I was in danger of creating a trench in the riverbank so deep that I'd fall all the way through to the Indian Ocean.

I glanced at my watch again, though I knew it only served to make me more nervous. Why did I keep torturing myself? It wasn't like time was going to flow backward and the rafting group would magically not be late anymore.

For the umpteenth time, I ran through all the safety precautions we always took—everything from daily inspections of the gear to the emergency rafts we had stashed along the stretch of river we run. No matter how many times I ran through the list, it didn't calm me.

The handheld radio clipped to my waist crackled. "Alex?" Daniel's voice said just as my hand wrapped around the hard, black plastic of the radio.

"Yeah."

"Any sign of them yet?"

I swallowed and looked up the river, still devoid of people or rafts. "Not yet."

I felt like I might hurl. My stomach had been in painful, twisting knots for hours. I hadn't even been able to eat breakfast this morning. Food held about as much appeal at the moment as taking a flying leap off the top of Cooley Mountain.

How was I going to be able to do this job for another summer before I could escape? It seemed that the more time that elapsed between Dad's death and the present, the more my hatred of the river built. Shouldn't it be the other way around? Shouldn't it fade with time? But it didn't. As it aged, it grew, curled itself around me and through me. The thought of running the river again caused an instinctive recoil, much like the idea of touching a flame. You simply didn't do either, because you knew the outcome could be nothing but bad.

The river surged past me, in its excited mood today after being fed by the rain the night before. But I imagined how it had behaved along the rapids upriver, crashing against the rocks in wild abandon, like a junkie on speed.

I redirected my gaze to the bright, blue sky. It had turned out to be a gorgeous day with that scent of rain-soaked forest I liked so much permeating the air. If only three rafts full of happy, safe rafters would float into view.

But when I looked at the river again, that wasn't what I saw floating toward me. Ignoring my fear of the water, I waded into the shallows and snatched the hat from the current. Tommy's distinctive tie-dyed bucket hat.

Oh God. The dream—it was real.

My heart banged painfully against my chest, and my lungs seized up as if they'd been dipped in concrete. Sean. Why hadn't I told him how I felt? That I was sorry for all those horrible things I'd said last summer? That none of them were true?

Laughter made me look up. Tommy was about to fall out of the lead raft because he was laughing so hard. All I could do was stare in disbelief—that everyone appeared to be okay, that Tommy thought this was a funny thing to joke about.

"You should have seen your face," Tommy said as he directed the raft past where I was standing, to the takeout point.

The passing of another raft, this one guided by Sean, drew my attention. But Sean wasn't looking at me. His furious gaze was fixed firmly on Tommy. In fact, he appeared on the verge of wringing the neck of one of the queen's subjects.

I came out of whatever weird, frozen shock I was in and started backing up on shaking legs toward shore, away from the cold, grasping water that wanted to pull me along with it on its journey downriver. I turned, gripping the dripping hat tightly in my hand. With each slogging step I made back toward shore, my anxiety was increasingly replaced by anger. I had to remind myself that Tommy was new here, that he might not have yet heard about Dad's accident. I mean, our family didn't talk about it. Still, that didn't dispel my desire to scream at him. I fought the urge to beat him with his wet hat for scaring me so much that my internal organs were still quaking.

But I couldn't, not in front of the guests. I might want to leave the rafting business soon, but it was still my family's source of income. I couldn't run off business by acting like a lunatic.

Somehow I pulled myself together enough to greet the guests when I stepped out onto the sandy edge of the river. "Sorry Mother Nature didn't cooperate for your trip."

"I might be soaked, but I still had a great time," a tall, thin, fortyish man said. His buddies nodded their agreement.

"Yeah, it rained like crazy last night. But this morning while we were waiting for the water to go down a bit, the sunrise was gorgeous," a tiny woman offered, her eyes bright with postrafting excitement.

For a moment, I envied them. Even though the river was no longer my dear friend, I still remembered the glory days of our friendship. Remembered that fantastic sense of being truly free and meeting the wildness of Mother Nature and laughing alongside her.

My jangled nerves calmed a bit as I dived into the familiar work of storing the rafts and gear. The takeout was so busy with activity that I appeared to be the only one who noticed that Sean had pulled Tommy several yards away and was right up in his face. I really should have separated them, but I didn't want to draw the guests' attention to the altercation. Plus, a voice inside me said that Sean had to care about me, at least a little, to go after Tommy for his ill-advised prank.

Once we had everything stored on the trailer and the guests were loaded in the van, their chatter masked any tension between Sean and Tommy. Chad, in the seat opposite mine, was quiet as well. I kept my eyes on the road and listened to the guests' conversation, focusing on their upbeat moods rather than the reason the rest of us weren't speaking. We were lucky the guests had a great time, or this ride back would have been even more uncomfortable.

Once we arrived at the office, I pulled into the gravel parking lot and slid out my door. I said goodbye to the guests and went inside to trade places with Daniel. I found him sitting at my desk, doing something on the computer. Mala was perched cross-legged atop the desk, chattering like some type of talkative tropical bird. Daniel sat with his chin-length blond hair hiding his face from Mala, but that didn't deter her monologue.

"I see you found the Tardy Boys," Mala said as she glanced at me.

My miserable morning must have been written across my face, because her expression changed to one of concern. "What's wrong?"

"Nothing." I waved her off, wanting to forget about the entire episode. "Daniel, can you go help them unload?"

"Sure." He jumped up and almost sprinted for the door. He looked so thankful to be free of Mala Central that I nearly laughed despite my horrible morning.

"Have you been talking poor Daniel's ear off? No wonder the guy zipped out."

"Ha-ha. He was holding down the fort alone. Who else was I supposed to talk to?"

"I don't think constant jabbering is on Daniel's Most Wanted list."

"The boy needs to liven up a bit. I came in here and found him reading *Crime and Punishment*." She lifted the heavy tome from the desk beside her and shook it like it was evil incarnate. "I mean, seriously—Dostoyevsky? In the summer!" She dropped the book back onto the desk as if it might contaminate her.

Mala slipped off the desk and shook her head in disbelief as she headed for the restroom.

I sank into the desk chair and stared at the copy of *Crime and Punishment*. My mood was causing me to lose my grip on reality, because I imagined the title staring up at me, taunting me. I turned the book over and leaned back in the chair. I closed my eyes and took several long breaths. Unfortunately, the maelstrom wouldn't vacate my head. Images of the book, then Dad, kept bumping into each other, until I was pulled back to the month before Dad had shipped off overseas. It was the day when I'd been assigned to read Alex Haley's *Roots* in my advanced English class.

I'd thunked my way in through the side door of our house and dropped my book bag onto the kitchen table with great drama. Dad had looked up from where he was washing his hands at the sink.

"It's book review time in Golden Bend."

He raised his eyebrow. "And that's a problem? You like to read."

"Yes, when it's cold outside." I looked with longing out the window above the sink. Spring had arrived, and I was being kept from enjoying it fully.

Dad turned toward me as he dried his hands on a dish towel. "What do you have to read? Can't be that bad."

"*Roots*. It's nine hundred pages long!"

Dad pasted on a feigned expression of shock before smiling. "That's a good book."

I looked at my dad in disbelief. "You've read it?" Dad's reading ran more to *Outside Magazine* and Larry McMurtry westerns.

He gave me a sheepish expression. "I watched the miniseries. Does that count?"

"Uh, no." I stalked to the fridge and grabbed a bottle of pineapple-orange juice. "I want to go rafting with you this weekend, not be stuck here reading."

Dad ruffled my dark, wavy hair. "School will be over before you know it. We'll have the entire summer to spend on the river."

Two days later, he received word that his National Guard unit was being activated and sent to parts unknown. It didn't take a genius to figure out he was headed someplace sandy, hot, and dangerous.

The screen door at the front of the office opened, the squeaky springs jerking me back to the present. Tommy came in, looking contrite. Even though I didn't want to have the conversation I sensed was coming, I was thankful he'd pulled me out of the past. Away from those days when I'd still thought my future lay with the river and Cooley Mountain Whitewater.

"What's up with him?" Mala said under her breath as she passed in front of me.

Tommy walked toward us, and I would have sworn he'd be twisting his cap in his hands if I didn't still have it. "Alex, can I talk to you for a minute?"

Mala gave me the "you're so going to tell me about this later" eye and wandered over to the gift shop side of the building. To keep from looking at Tommy, I watched as she plucked up an individual-size bag of dried apricots.

Having finished with the guests and the gear, the rest of the guys filed in and headed straight for the fridge to retrieve drinks. I deliberately didn't make eye contact with any of them. I didn't want to see their pity or discomfort.

"I'm sorry about the hat joke," Tommy said, drawing my attention back to him. "I had no idea about your dad."

I nodded, afraid that if I spoke my voice would crack. The sickening fear I'd felt when that hat had floated into view surged through me again before calming.

"I want to make it up to you," he said as he rounded the counter that bisected the eastern half of the building between the front and back doors.

"That's not necessary."

"Still, I want to." He moved even closer and leaned against the edge of the desk. "We could hang out after work, have a cookout at the beach."

The "beach" was a sandy bend in the river that had seen everything from harmless cookouts to drunken orgies. An all-purpose gathering place.

I glanced across the room to where Sean wasn't looking at me. "I don't think so."

"Come on, we'll make it a group outing. Everyone can

come." He slapped Daniel on the back as he passed by with a root beer and a Snickers bar. "It'll be fun."

"That's a great idea," Mala said as she plopped back down on the opposite side of the desk and tossed an apricot into her mouth. "We'll be there." She gave me a look that said not to argue.

"Cool!" Tommy said. "Who's in?"

Chad and Daniel said they were, and I sensed, more than saw, a nod from Sean. I couldn't figure out why he'd agreed after his altercation with Tommy.

Well, it looked like everyone else had just decided the fate of my afternoon. Another glance at Sean as he opened a can of Coke made my heart do that little extra boom-boom. I ignored the fact that he had yet to make eye contact with me all morning. Instead, I tried to convince myself that this cookout was a great idea. I had decided I wanted to have fun with my friends this summer, right?

Mala smacked the back of her hand against my upper arm, and I uttered a "me" just to make it official. Mala smiled wide, very pleased with herself. The girl really did know how to enjoy life to its fullest. I thought maybe I'd try to emulate her this summer, though I didn't think there was any danger of me taking away her Queen of the Party crown.

The snack delivery truck pulled up outside. I eyeballed all my coworkers, including my wide-grinning cousin. "Well, if we're going to party later, you losers better get to work." I grabbed Tommy's still-wet hat and threw it at him. It hit his yellow Cooley Mountain Whitewater T-shirt right in the middle of his chest, making a *splat* sound.

Tommy clutched the hat, threw up a salute, then headed out the door, laughing.

I caught Sean's eye for a brief moment as he trailed the other guys out the door. I couldn't peg the expression he gave me. As usual, he proved unreadable. My stomach knotted. Was this impromptu party a way for me to make amends with him or a huge, honking mistake?

CHAPTER 5

I stared at the bright red, Victoria's Secret push-up bra that hung from Mala's outstretched finger.

"Put it on," she said.

"Tell me again why I need to change bras to go to a cookout with guys we work with every day."

"Because you've got a severe case of the yearnings for one of them."

"Oh yeah. That's right." I eyed my cousin and her lingerie offering. "Why'd you change your mind?"

"About what?"

"Sean. One day you want me to forget about him, and the next you want me to get sexy for him."

"Yeah, well, it took about five minutes of watching you when he's anywhere nearby to figure out the first wasn't going to happen anytime soon." She twirled the bra around the end of her finger. "So I figure full steam ahead is better than pining on the sidelines."

"I doubt a bra is going to suddenly make everything better between me and Sean."

"Do not underestimate the power of Vicki. Besides, even

if things with Sean go nowhere, it'll be fun to see the rest of the guys' stunned expressions when you show up with major bazooms."

I snorted as I took the bra and headed into the bathroom. "I'm not on an all-out campaign to win him back, you know. Like you said, he may not even be interested anymore."

"You won't know until you try."

"I know. But no obvious gestures to push us together, okay?" I paused to switch bras, then fluffed my hair a little. Most of the time I wore it up in a ponytail, but if I was going with the sexy boobs, why not the sexy hair, too?

When I walked back into the bedroom, Mala gave me the thumbs-up. "Now if that doesn't get the boy's attention, he doesn't have a heartbeat. Or other interesting body parts."

"I'm not trying to seduce him, goofball."

"Why not? With that lean, muscled body, I bet he'd be really good."

The thought of sex with Sean made me flush all over. I shared a lot with Mala, but I'd never uttered a word about the hot dreams I'd had about Sean. Let's just say they were way nicer than my recurring nightmares.

Mala crossed her arms and looked at me. "You do want him back, right?"

"Yeah . . . I mean, well, yes. I do. But I said a lot of awful things before. I'm not going to pretend that didn't happen. I just . . . I want to take it slow, in case . . ." I couldn't utter the words *he's moved on* aloud.

Mala hugged me, and I hugged her back. It had always

been great to have my cousin be my best friend too, even when we'd fought or disagreed.

"I know ways to figure out what guys are thinking. Just leave everything to me." With that, she bounced toward the door and giggled.

"Mala!" I knew that gleam in her bright blue eyes.

"Don't worry so much. I'm not luring you both to a boudoir in the woods. The males of our species are just dense sometimes, and it's up to us to make the first move."

Aunt Charlotte stopped by the open door to Mala's room. Even in jeans and a T-shirt from the coffee shop she owned, she looked elegant. Looking at her chin-length, straight blonde hair and bright blue eyes gave me a glimpse of what Mala might look like in twenty years. Still stunning.

"Where are you girls off to?" she asked.

"A cookout," Mala said as she slipped her feet into a cute pair of flip-flops adorned with fake jewels. Terrible shoes for trekking down to the river through the woods, but so very Mala.

My aunt looked at me as she nodded toward Mala. "Make sure this one stays out of trouble."

"Nice, Mom," Mala said as she stood and stalked toward the door. "Thanks for the vote of confidence." She brushed past her mom and headed toward the stairs to the lower level.

I directed an apologetic smile at my dad's sister and followed Mala out of the house to my Jeep.

"What was that about?" I asked as I caught up to her.

"Nothing." Mala jerked the passenger door open and hopped into her seat.

O-kay.

As we headed to the river, my own concerns returned and pinged around in my head. "What if Sean really is seeing that girl?" The thought escaped my mouth before I realized it.

"Then we'll find the fat ho and pluck her eyebrows out."

I snorted, then shot her a "seriously" look. "A bit extreme, perhaps?"

"Depends." She turned in her seat so that her back was against the passenger door. "As Grandma says, we'll cross that bridge when we come to it. First, we scope out the situation."

"I wonder sometimes if our relationship has turned into something more in my memory than it really ever was." I paused to consider that possibility. "How lame is that?"

"You didn't see his face when he looked at you the day he left. That boy loved you."

"Loved. Maybe. But I ruined it." My voice caught.

"Sean's a smart guy. He has to know you were grieving."

"Then why didn't he call me during all the months since then?"

"You both had phones, sweets."

She had a point, but it hurt to hear it.

"I picked up the phone a few times."

"Doesn't count unless you dial the numbers."

But the thought of him hanging up on me had just been too much to consider when my emotions were already so raw. So I'd avoided the possibility. Months had gone by, and it had become easier to keep avoiding the whole situation. It wasn't like I had to work side by side with him every day. He was out of sight, if not out of mind.

When we arrived at the pull-off area near the river, Mala grabbed my arm before I could get out of the Jeep.

"Remember, you're here to have fun with your friends. Leave everything that's in the past back there where it belongs and just see what develops."

I considered her words for a moment, then nodded. "You're right. Let's party." The words felt foreign even though I'd tried my very best to mean them.

We meandered along the path worn among the pines, a route most of my classmates could have navigated blind-folded. In a town of two thousand people, you made your own entertainment, and riverside parties were a perennial favorite.

"Crap!" Mala lifted her foot and pulled a pine twig from where it'd slipped between her foot and her flip-flop. She eyed me as she pitched the offending tree part to the right of the path. "Not one word about my choice of shoes."

I lifted my hands. "Did I say anything?"

"You didn't have to. I saw that 'I'm about to impart woodsy wisdom' look on your face."

I shook my head and walked past her. If she didn't use her common sense, why should I care?

When we finally made our way through the woods to the beach, we found that the guys had started a bonfire, a really large one. It crackled and sent little sparks flying into the air. I stood at the top of the hill above them and placed my hands on my hips. "Are you all planning on roasting the Oscar Mayer Wienermobile?"

Tommy looked up, smiled as wide as the Cheshire cat, and tossed me a bottle of beer. Mala grabbed a beer of her own and winked at me as she moved into the circle of guys, closer to Sean. My resolve to act as if I didn't have a care in the world—or at least Colorado—weakened a little.

No, I wouldn't think about how Mala's plans often backfired. I wouldn't think about the ginormous cooler of beer perched on the beach like a pirate's treasure chest and how it made me nervous to have alcohol near the river. I was here to have fun, and that's what I planned to do. I wouldn't be the party pooper.

Tommy switched the CDs in the player perched next to the cooler. As he stepped away, the energetic notes of "In the Shadows" by the Rasmus filled the air. A month ago, I hadn't heard of the Rasmus, but the Finnish band was just one European group Tommy was determined to introduce us all to this summer.

Chad pulled two sticks with hog dogs on them out of the fire. He turned to Sean, who stepped near the fire a bit before me. "Which one you want?"

Sean glanced at me for a split second, then wrapped his hand around the stick holding the less-burned hot dog. I knew I shouldn't read any meaning into his actions, especially not until I had the chance to apologize. But part of me wondered if he'd left the blackened hot dog for me because he remembered that was how I liked them.

Mala bumped her shoulder into mine. "Careful. You're about to drool on yourself."

I deliberately pressed my lips together and turned my attention to Chad. "Thanks," I said as I took my charcoal dog. I retreated to a log on the opposite side of the fire from Sean, trying to ignore the need to drag him away from all these people so we could talk in private. Instead, I slipped off my athletic mules and dug my toes into the thick layer of sand.

As we ate hot dogs and then gooey, delicious s'mores, we laughed about the antics of some of our past rafting customers.

"I still about pee myself every time I think of Paris and Nicole," Chad said.

Mala put out her hand. "Oh no, not that story. I hurt myself laughing every time I hear it," she said.

"Paris and Nicole?" Tommy asked.

"Not the real ones," I said. "There were these two girls, twins, who were on a trip with their boyfriends. Let's just say that tent walls are thin, and none of us got any sleep."

Mala snorted. "I'll never get that sound out of my head."

Chad took it upon himself to reenact the wild-animal sounds of the sex-crazed couples, and we all lost it. I laughed so hard I had to hold my side and wipe the tears from my eyes.

"When I was running the Ocoee back in Tennessee, there was this dude who ran the river naked," Daniel said. "He was writing some book called *Naked Sports* or something."

"Was he hot?" Mala asked, then took a swig of her beer.

"Naked dudes, not really my thing. Now if it'd been Jessica Alba, it'd be a different story."

"I doubt you'd take your nose out of a book long enough to see Jessica and her ta-tas float by."

"At least I read something besides *The Art of Flirting*."

Mala stuck her tongue out at Daniel.

New bottles of beer were passed around the circle. I hesitated, glanced at the river as the shadows began gathering in spots on the far shore, before taking a bottle for myself.

"Do you remember that guy from Chicago, the one who proposed to his girlfriend in the middle of the trip?" Sean asked as he tossed small sticks into the fire.

"Barry Stephenson," Daniel said and shook his head. "Poor sap. There's a guy who should have just stuck to books instead of women."

We each tossed out part of the story about Barry, who had saved for a year to bring his girlfriend on a trip to Colorado to propose. Only his plan didn't go quite as he'd hoped. During a peaceful part of the trip downriver, he'd pulled out a diamond ring and asked her to marry him. When she'd proceeded to tell him that she'd been sleeping with his brother, Barry had tossed the ring into the river, then jumped overboard.

"The last we saw of him was as he pulled his soaking-wet self onto the riverbank and headed through the forest," Chad said.

"Harsh," Tommy said as he grabbed his third beer.

I caught Sean's eye and wondered about the nameless girl in Denver. Had he been sleeping with her the way Barry's girlfriend had with his brother?

"How about some truth or dare?" Mala asked.

Normally, truth or dare with Mala was a very bad idea, but I said, "Sure." Anything to not think about Sean with some other girl.

As the hilarity of the game built, I began to relax. The fire crackled, sending smoke and embers curling into the air. It kept the warmth of our circle constant even though the air cooled more the closer the sun dipped toward the western horizon. Already the sun wasn't visible from our spot down by the river. The shadows edged closer as if they were night creatures curious about the humans in their midst.

This felt like old times during the summers before Dad got called up for National Guard duty. I laughed when Sean forced Tommy to tell the truth about how long he breast-fed. And when Chad took Tommy's dare and did a flying belly flop from the top of the hill into the river, drawing a collective "Ow!" from all of us. When it was my turn, I chose truth. Mala gave me her mischievous look and asked, "When was the last time you had a sex dream?"

Oh, I was so going to get her back. "I don't remember my dreams."

"That's such a lie." Mala gave me an accusatory look, like she couldn't believe I had the gall to lie during truth or dare.

Did I mention that Mala attacked this game with the gusto of soldiers storming a beachhead, much to my annoyance?

Daniel was the last up. He had to go with dare, since he'd chosen truth the previous time around.

Mala rubbed her hands together like an evil mastermind in a cartoon. "Let's see. Okay, I've got it! Daniel, you've got to strip down—totally—and swim across the river and back."

I bet he wished he hadn't told the naked-rafter story now.

Daniel eyed Mala, his eyes narrowed a bit as if the gears were working furiously in his head to figure a way out of the situation. A hint of a smile tugged at the edges of his lips.

"That anxious to see me naked, huh?" he asked.

I snorted beer out my nose, not only at Mala getting burned but that it was by Daniel. Reserved, studious Daniel had a snarky side after all.

For a brief moment, Mala looked as surprised as the rest of us, her eyes widening. But then she crossed her arms and gave Daniel a challenging look. "Honey, if you've got any-thing worth seeing, start shucking."

The rest of the guys hooted with laughter. Daniel just shook his head, indicating there would be no tossing of clothes anytime soon.

Mala pumped her hand in victory. "I still totally rule this game."

When Tommy got up and pulled more beer from the cooler for all of us, he weaved. I had to blink a few times myself to try to clear my vision. The world had skewed, and I faintly realized I was getting a pretty good buzz.

After a few more swigs of beer had us snorting and laugh-ing at just about everything, Tommy produced an empty bot-tle and pronounced it time to play spin the bottle.

"Brilliant idea!" Mala said in a really bad British accent,

sounding like she was imitating those guys in the Guinness commercials.

I couldn't help it. I'd drunk enough to let my guard down, so I looked over at Sean. He was leaning back on his hands with his long legs stretched out and crossed at the ankles. And he was staring right at me. I couldn't read his expression. Was that because he was being his normal unreadable self, or were my senses more dulled than I thought from the drinking? I blinked, slowly, but he was still there, wavering in my vision. Maybe it was the smoke and heat waves from the fire creating the illusion that he wasn't quite in focus.

I was aware enough to realize that I had stared at him too long. I imagined him standing and trampling all over my feelings, twisting them into the sand so they could be washed away by the river. The beer churned in my stomach, dancing an unpleasant tango with the hot dog.

"Um, the odds seem a little off to you?" I asked Mala as I blinked several more times to refocus on her face, closer to mine than Sean's had been.

"Are you joking?" Tommy asked. "The odds are great."

I glanced at Tommy, who winked at me. He was like one of those English rakes in romance novels, a mixture of naughtiness and fun.

"You would say that. There are four of you," I said as I swept my hand to encompass all of the guys.

"Like he said, great odds," Chad said, and smiled wide.

I rolled my eyes at him then immediately regretted it, afraid they'd get stuck in midroll.

I didn't particularly want to kiss any of the guys besides Sean, and I was afraid if my spin landed on him he'd refuse and just walk away. Talk about pain and humiliation. I couldn't look at him to gauge his reaction, but he hadn't voiced an objection. Was that a good sign? Did he hope to have an excuse to kiss me again? But what if he was dating someone? Did I want a guy who went around randomly kissing girls while dating someone else?

My head throbbed at the endless questions. I hated all this uncertainty. I looked at Sean and noticed him scooting in closer in the circle, as was everyone else. He glanced my direction, and I swore I saw a small smile on his lips. What was that for?

"I don't know what the problem is," Tommy said. "You girls have the good end of the deal. You have a fifty-fifty chance of kissing a hot stud each time the bottle stops."

I smacked Tommy's arm.

"Oh, my arm, my arm," he wailed in dramatic fashion. "I've been attacked by a crazy woman."

His dramatics set off a new wave of hooting and laughing. Even I got caught up in it and forgot my reservations about kissing my coworkers. The laughter still echoed down the river as the bottle started spinning. I held my breath until Chad got matched up with Mala.

"Come on, Big Mouth. Let's see if you live up to your own hype," Mala said as she moved in for a kiss. She was in full-on flirt mode, so she gave Chad a bit more than a peck.

Tommy egged on the kiss by cheering as if he were at a

ball game. Sean shook his head while smiling. Daniel read-justed his stance, and I wondered if he was uncomfortable and thinking about bolting.

Next up was Tommy, and I squirmed a little as the bottle spun. But, again, Mala was the prize of the spin. Tommy leaned across me to reach my cousin and met the enthusias-tic kiss with gusto. Either Mala had been lying about liking Tommy in a romantic way, or she had a pretty good buzz going too.

When they broke the kiss, Mala said, "Not bad, British boy."

He puffed up like guys do, looking quite proud of him-self. "I get to kiss the lovely Alex next, and I can go back to England a happy man."

A quick look at Sean showed him sitting perfectly still, staring at the bottle in the center of our circle. Why couldn't he wear his emotions out in the open? Didn't he realize that I needed to know what was going on in that head of his? Had he had any reaction at all to Tommy saying he wanted to kiss me?

Daniel ended up not making a frantic retreat, but he didn't make eye contact with Mala or me either. I wondered which of us he considered less embarrassing to kiss. He leaned forward to spin, his longish blond hair falling to hide his face. When the top of the bottle stopped closest to me, I forced myself not to utter a sound of disappointment or hazard a glance at Sean. I couldn't stand the thought that his expression might show he didn't care one way or the other.

Looking as uncomfortable as I felt, Daniel half-crawled

toward me and barely touched his lips to mine. I lasted for a millisecond before pulling away.

"Dude, lame," Chad said.

In response, Daniel punched him in the arm. Mala shifted beside me but didn't say anything. Maybe the beer was finally hitting her.

When I realized it was now my turn to spin, nervousness welled up and threatened to make me run for the woods. Instead, I reached my hand forward and touched the bottle. I swallowed and licked my lips, willing the bottle to work some magic.

"Come on, love," Tommy teased. "Don't keep me in suspense. My heart can't take it."

I spun, and sure enough, when it stopped, it was pointing toward Tommy. Before I could move, he was leaning toward me and attempting a repeat of the kiss he'd given me before the raft trip. When he tried to French me, I pulled away, my cheeks flaming. I passed the bottle on to Mala, who oddly wouldn't meet my eye.

Mala stretched out her long, tanned arm, grabbed the brown bottle, and spun it with more force than anyone so far. What was up with her?

I watched the revolutions, and before the bottle stopped I knew where it was going to be pointing. The mouth of the bottle came to rest facing Sean. I wanted to scream, "No!" Instead, I sat in silence as Mala leaned over, presenting her ample cleavage for inspection. Of course time slowed to add to my agony as she gave Sean a kiss just as enthusiastic as those she'd given Chad and Tommy. My fists clenched when

I thought she might be slipping him a little tongue. What the hell? Was this her idea of helping me get back with Sean? And why wasn't he pulling away? Damn, it was the kiss that wouldn't end!

When they finally, eons later, ended the kiss, I jerked my gaze away. I didn't want to chance seeing something on Sean's face I couldn't handle. After all, what guy wouldn't get turned on if Mala were virtually in his lap?

I sat and stewed, biting the inside of my cheek, my head pounding more as the second round started. No matter how many guys Mala kissed, I wasn't able to wipe away the image of her and Sean together. Leave everything to her, huh? Some freakin' fantastic win-back-Sean-for-me plan this was.

By the time the bottle was nearly back to me, I couldn't sit there anymore, pretending that I was having a good time. I had to get away before I embarrassed myself. I felt like I was toeing a microscopic line between puking and letting my feelings for Sean spill out in an embarrassing flood. I couldn't let myself stumble through an apology while I was half drunk and upset. And not in front of all these people.

As Mala and Chad shared another kiss, the overwhelming need to flee slammed into me. Fog invaded my brain, making it hard to think clearly. I stumbled to my feet and almost tipped toward the fire. It seemed fitting, since I felt like I was going up in flames anyway. Instead of attracting Sean, the borrowed Victoria's Secret bra constricted my breathing, making my head swim.

"What's wrong?" Tommy asked and started to stand. He

tilted toward the fire until Chad grabbed his arm and pulled him back down.

I held out my hand, palm out, and shook my head. Big mistake. My vision blurred, which made my stomach turn flips. "Nothing."

Everything.

"Alex?" Sean sounded concerned, but I couldn't let myself believe it. Not when I wasn't sure what I was seeing or hearing was really happening. Somehow, hearing that concern from him made everything worse.

Get away, get away, get away.

I mumbled the word *beer* as I took a few more shaky steps away from the fire. Let them think I couldn't hold my alcohol. I didn't care anymore. I looked through the heat waves from the fire toward Sean. Again, I couldn't decipher his expression. But I thought he might be about to get to his feet, so I turned and headed toward the trees at the top of the riverbank. As I entered the forest, the light faded some. I weaved from tree to tree, reaching out to steady myself against the rough bark of each.

I vaguely realized I should be paying attention to where I was going, so I didn't get lost or trip off a cliff into the river. But all I could think about was that unreadable flicker in Sean's eyes as he'd watched me through the fire.

CHAPTER 6

I kept walking until I moved out of visual and hearing range of my friends. The pine trees around me scented the summery air. My slight climb in elevation away from the river alleviated the cool dampness I'd felt enveloping me before I'd left the beach. It also helped clear my head a little, though my head still swam if I turned it too quickly.

I picked my way through the forest, moving in and out of shady areas, until I came to a rocky outcropping, one of countless such vantage points above the river. I sat down on the warm rocks.

The sun dipped behind the mountains, casting large sections of the canyons in deeper shadow. I closed my eyes, breathed deeply, and focused on the sound of the rushing river below. Once that sound had soothed me, and I longed for that feeling again.

How many times had I sat on a ledge much like this on my grandparents' ranch and watched rafters and kayakers float down the river? I smiled at a memory of Sean and me sitting on that cliff when we were about twelve.

"Ah, look at this, mates," Sean had said in an almost-perfect imitation of Steve Irwin, the Crocodile Hunter. "I haven't seen a specimen like this in, oh, probably twenty minutes. But this one is nearly perfect. Ask me what it is."

I had laughed as I'd watched a middle-aged man far below us hang on to the rope around the edge of the raft for dear life. "What is it?"

"The not-so-rare Naturus Clueless," the younger version of Sean said in my head, taking me back nearly five years.

My younger self snorted at the fake name, obviously a product of our teacher Mrs. Brandon's introduction to binomial nomenclature the week before. "You've been doing too much science homework again."

Sean leaned back on his palms. "You have to admit, it comes in handy."

I watched the tourists float out of sight. "True. Doesn't it seem weird that there are people who are so uncomfortable out in nature?"

"Yeah. Guess they'd make fun of us if we got plunked down in the middle of L.A., though."

"Good thing that's not too likely. I can't imagine living somewhere else."

"Me neither."

The breeze stirred the treetops above me, returning me to the present and to the realization of how wrong we'd been. Sean now spent most of his year in Denver, and I'd be leaving Golden Bend as soon as I graduated. I still doubted I'd land in L.A., but it would certainly be someplace that didn't remind me of Colorado—especially if there proved to be no hope of Sean and me getting back together.

Even the peaceful sound of the wind caressing the pine needles couldn't keep the image of Mala kissing Sean out of my head for long. She didn't mean anything by it, of course. Right? After all, she was way tipsy and either had drunk way more than I had or didn't hold her alcohol as well. But that didn't make the image of her mouth claiming Sean's any less painful. How was I going to find out if he still liked me at all if I couldn't even manage to look at him for more than a few seconds?

The brush of footsteps sounded through the trees. I glanced over my shoulder as Sean rounded a thicker stand of pines. I jerked my gaze back toward the river, the sudden movement making my head throb. I closed my eyes, waited for the throbbing to ease and my stomach to settle. With my eyes closed, the sound of Sean's footsteps magnified. I wondered if it was possible for memories of a person to conjure him in the present.

"Kissing Tommy couldn't have been so bad that you're contemplating jumping."

I turned my head more slowly this time. Even buzzed, I could learn a lesson. Sean stood there, leaning against a tree with his arms crossed. Tall, gorgeous, tempting me to run my fingers through his sun-streaked hair. Even more startling than him following me was the fact that he was teasing me. I didn't know how to handle it or what it meant.

"I needed to call my grandma; I didn't want her to hear what was going on," I lied.

"That you were hanging out with your friends."

"That those friends are halfway to drunk."

Sean laughed and walked toward me. "There's no way for her to know, since there's no cell reception down here." He held his phone where I could see the display showing no bars and the words *No Service*, effectively calling me a liar. Why hadn't I thought of that?

"You give yourself away, you know." He sat on the far end of the rock, and I tried to act normal, as if my heart wasn't about to bruise itself beating against my rib cage.

"What do you mean?"

"When you try to lie, your eyes get all wide." He widened his eyes in imitation.

"I don't look like that!"

"You do." He smiled, stealing more of my ability to think clearly. Combine alcohol with Sean actually talking to me again, and I was a lost cause.

I threw up my hands. "You caught me." Maybe Sean and I needed to learn to be friends again before we could be anything more—if we'd ever be anything more again. I wasn't going to rush things and ruin what might be my only chance to have Sean back in my life.

"So, what's really up?" he asked.

I turned my gaze toward the canyon wall on the opposite side of the river, almost completely in shadow now. I didn't want him to see my telltale wide eyes. "The beer, the noise, everything was just giving me a headache. I wanted to get away for a bit."

"And you couldn't just say that?"

"And be the world's biggest wuss? Not likely." I threw in a little laugh for effect. It felt fake and awkward, like our relationship was stuck in some sort of foggy netherworld between friendship and complete strangers.

"So, how's your headache now?"

Was it my imagination, or had he just inflected the word *headache* in such a way as to call me on my line of bull? Gah, I was in a no-win situation here, perched on a cliff and being expertly grilled by the guy whose recent lip lock had driven me here in the first place.

"Better."

"Good." He sat in silence probably five feet away, as if we were holding down opposite ends of the large rock slab. Once we would have sat shoulder to shoulder, even before there'd been anything romantic between us. But now I found it hard to sit still.

Part of me wanted to blurt out everything, that I was sorry, that I wanted to start over, and beg for his forgiveness. But a bigger part warned me to take it slowly. Baby steps. Plus, I felt like I might puke at any moment. It'd be my luck to start apologizing, then have to go heave in the bushes.

And there was that whole kissing-Mala vision still burning my corneas.

"At least you seem to be holding your booze better than Mala," he said. "Put a little beer down her, and suddenly she loves everyone." He laughed like it was all a big joke.

Could I tell him after all?

"Still, it's fun to hang out with everyone," he said. "I've missed my friends here."

Friends. The word echoed in my head. Was that what he considered me now? Just a friend?

The thought of apologizing died in me.

I picked up a pebble and pitched it out over the river, wishing I could get rid of the ache inside me as easily.

"I see you still throw like a girl."

The familiarity of the old but friendly argument tugged at me, but I didn't feel like rising to the bait today. "Maybe that's because I am a girl."

Silence met my response before Sean tossed a pebble over the edge, not putting any strength behind it. "You okay?"

What a loaded question. Hell, no, I wasn't okay. "Yeah. Just tired."

We sat in silence. My buzz faded a little, making me more aware of the sound of the water flowing against rocks below and the scurrying of some small animal in the woods. That cool scent of evening was beginning to drift out of the thicker parts of the forest.

"You remember when we used to sit like this and make up stories about the people rafting by?" Sean asked.

I ventured a glance at him and smiled a little. "Weird. I was just thinking about that before you showed up." A pang pulled at my chest that we both had the same memory nearly at the same time.

A memory from when we were "just friends."

"Hard to forget some of those people."

Not nearly as difficult as forgetting Sean. "Yeah." My brain felt like it was slogging through wet cement, trying to put together a decent response to everything Sean said, every gesture or movement he made.

That uncomfortable silence that I couldn't have imagined

between us only a year ago descended again, making me desperate to fill it.

"So, wanna go back and see who Mala's attacking now? Or if Tommy has managed to fall into the fire?"

Sean shrugged. "If your 'headache' is better."

He did say *headache* differently. He was teasing me!

I couldn't describe how good that felt.

We didn't say anything as we picked our way through the woods back toward the river, but that was okay. Our conversation back on the cliff had been a nice, if awkward, first step. I just had to figure out what the best next step was.

When we reached the beach, our friends seemed excited about something. When Mala spotted us, she ran forward, squealing and clapping her hands, the entire incident with the kisses evidently forgotten.

"We have the best idea!" she said.

"Really?" My internal warning system against Mala's great ideas sounded in my head. Sure, I'd gone along with many of them because, despite her faults, Mala was a lot of fun.

"Yeah. This bonfire was such a good time, we should have a bigger party. A huge party!" She extended her arms out from her, indicating some picture of "huge" in her mind. "Oh, and I know the perfect place. There's that old building a few miles from town. You know the one."

She gestured in the air, frustrated that the beer she'd consumed had affected her memory and ability to communicate.

"The old textile mill?" Chad asked.

"Yes!" she said and kissed him loudly on the cheek for helping her find the words.

Remember those warning bells in my head? Well, they were clanging like cathedral bells at the moment.

"I'm not breaking into the mill."

Mala waved away my concern. "Nobody uses it anymore. It just sits there getting dusty. And it's perfect."

"Perfect for getting us arrested."

"You're such a dud sometimes, Alex." Mala had that determined look on her face. "You need to lighten up."

"Come on," Tommy said as he draped his arm around my shoulders and the scent of his beer breath accosted me. "What's a little harmless fun?"

I glanced around at the others and saw that I was being cast as the lame-o buzzkill. Hey, it wasn't like I was against parties, only breaking and entering. Yeah, that looked fantastic on a college application. But a party, another opportunity to spend more time with Sean outside of work, time in which maybe he'd change his mind about being just friends? Excitement bubbled up at the idea.

"What about the barn instead?" I heard myself ask.

"What barn?" Tommy asked.

I caught Mala's gaze. "The one at the back of our grandparents' ranch."

Mala's eyes brightened. "Perfect!" She bounded forward and, continuing the theme of beer-induced love, planted a big kiss on my cheek. "I didn't think you had it in you."

What in me? Before I could ask what she meant, she'd already started ticking off ideas for the party on her manicured fingers. Had I created a monster?

I looked back at Sean, who had been silent on the subject, and he offered me a small smile. All of a sudden, giddiness made me want to bounce around, Tigger-like, too.

Hope blossomed inside me, then determination. Between now and the barn party, I planned to do what I could to make Sean like me as more than a friend again. And I'd build up my nerve and figure out the perfect way to tell him I was sorry about how things had ended between us before. How I still cared about him. That I didn't really blame him for my father's death.

CHAPTER 7

We hung out at the beach—eating warm, gooey s'mores, skipping rocks across the darkening surface of the water, letting the cooling mountain air caress our skin, and tossing out party ideas—until we were all sober and the quarter slice of moon had risen. As we traipsed back through the woods toward where we'd parked, Mala hooked her arm through mine.

"You should spend the night with me so Grandma and Grandpa don't find out you've been drinking."

"What about your parents?" Sure, Aunt Charlotte and Uncle Brad were more modern than our grandparents, but I doubted they'd overlook drinking. Especially since Uncle Brad was a lawyer and really had to respect the law.

"They won't even notice when we come in."

Her suggestion made sense, but I was still bothered enough by Mala's kiss with Sean that I really didn't want to spend the night with her tonight. I'd rather risk facing my grandparents with beer breath and being grounded. I cupped my hand in front of my mouth and exhaled. Hmm, most of the smell was gone anyway.

"I'm just going to go home and sleep it off." Well, not home. My single-story log house sat empty while Mom recuperated in Florida, and I was a long-term guest at my grandparents' house. Still, I wanted to spend the night there rather than with my cousin. I knew she likely hadn't meant anything by the kiss, but it still didn't alleviate the sense of betrayal. Hopefully everything would be better in the morning, but for right now I wanted to be alone.

I avoided giving Mala an answer until I pulled into her driveway. When I didn't turn off the Jeep's engine, she looked over at me.

"I'll see you in the morning," I said.

Without a word, she slipped out and hurried to the side door of her modern house, with its huge bank of windows looking out on the mountains. I could see my aunt and uncle sitting in the living room. True to Mala's assertion, they didn't even flinch when she entered the house.

I hoped I would be as lucky when I got home.

Miracle of miracles, I did make it in without having to face my grandparents. Luck had been on my side as I'd entered the house, berating myself for letting the meaningless kiss override my better judgment. I'd found a note from Grandma letting me know she and Grandpa had gone out to dinner with their longtime friends the Shaws.

But the evening had not been without consequence. This morning, I had the mother of all headaches and the urge to wear gigantic sunglasses, even indoors. I brushed my teeth and tongue for a good twenty minutes, trying to get rid of the extrafoul morning breath.

As I rinsed out my mouth, tidbits from the night before surfaced in my brain. The tale of the naked rafter, Daniel's unexpected response to Mala's dare, talking with Sean on the cliff. And then I remembered the barn party.

What an atrociously bad idea that had been. My gut told me to nix it as soon as possible and live with the party-pooper moniker if necessary. If this was how I felt after a simple bonfire with a few friends, I would feel like the dregs of death after a huge party. Not to mention that if we were caught, it'd be one more painful event for my grandparents to endure. My staying at their house already served as a constant reminder of why I wasn't in my own bedroom a few miles away.

But what about that smile Sean had given me last night amidst the party plans? Did he *really* want to remain just friends?

I'd have to come up with something else, maybe even get brave and plan an outing with only the two of us. My nerves and the remnants of the previous night nearly made me hurl.

Continuing in the miraculous vein, I made it through breakfast without tossing my bacon and toast, or having a big sign appear on my forehead proclaiming, "I was involved in much underage drinking last night." Grandma's humming and occasional glances at me made me feel like she was waiting for a confession, so I ate and bolted as quickly as I could.

When I reached the office, still wearing my sunglasses

to keep light at bay, I was in the mood to share my misery. I started to call Mala, not caring that she probably had an even bigger headache than I did. *Mala, the party's off*, I practiced in my head as I dialed. As the phone rang, I looked up. Sean stood there looking impossibly gorgeous in long cargo shorts and a white tee that made me yearn to run my hands over his chest. I hung up the phone and uttered an awkward, "Hey." I glanced down at the desk as I slid off my sunglasses, much to the displeasure of my eyeballs, before I returned my gaze to Sean.

He leaned against the front counter and gave me a crooked smile. "Feeling rough this morning?"

"That obvious, huh?"

"You're a little green."

From old habit, I stuck my tongue out at him. He laughed and headed for the cabinet where we kept snacks for the employees. He pulled out a honey bun. It was almost as if the past year hadn't happened—the bad or the good. Like we'd reverted to our pure friendship days.

"So I've got the music covered for the party. I used it as an excuse to go ahead and buy the system I've been looking at."

He bought a new stereo system? For the party? I ran my hand over my face. I couldn't cancel it now. Plus, he sounded like he was looking forward to it. Was that because he liked a good party, or was his reason more in line with mine? Maybe we could manage the party without my grandparents finding out. . . .

"That's cool," I muttered as I booted up the computer,

visions of dancing with Sean in some dark corner of the barn playing through my mind.

"Yeah, it should be loud enough to fill the barn, even with a lot of people there."

Sean chomped on his sugary breakfast and went to open the blinds at the front of the cabin. The streaming sunlight made me cover my eyes and moan.

"How do you not feel like total crap this morning?" I asked him.

"You're smaller than me. Less body weight. It hit you harder."

My headache took another beating when the door banged open again and Tommy strode in holding a clear, plastic pitcher of something I could only describe as disgustingly viscous.

"Never fear. I'm here bearing Tommy's hangover cure-all."

"What is that?" I asked, afraid of the answer.

"I can't divulge the secret recipe," he said as he poured a plastic cup of the goo and placed it in front of me. "But it is guaranteed to work."

My stomach rose to my throat, like it had the one and only time I rode the Tower of Terror at Disney World. With a painful swallow, I returned it to its proper area of my body. "If I drink that, I'll puke for days."

Tommy displayed mock affront. "I'm hurt. I come bearing my miracle cure, and you tell her she's not pretty."

"You sure that's fit for human consumption?" Sean asked, giving the goo a wary look.

"I've drunk it lots of times. It's an old English specialty."

"Make a habit of getting wasted, do ya?" Sean asked.

"I know how to have a good time." Tommy turned and winked at me. "And show others a good time in the process."

I would have rolled my eyes if I didn't think they'd pop out of my head. To direct the conversation away from Tommy's ever-present sexual innuendo, I braved putting my hand around the cup of pulverized greenness and brought it up to my mouth. Before I could think about it too much, I gulped it down in one swallow.

I slammed the cup down and started gagging. I stuck my tongue out and wiped at it ineffectively with a stray fast-food napkin. "That'll cure my hangover, all right—by killing me!" I stumbled to the fridge and grabbed a bottle of water, chugged some down. But I stopped when the water hit my stomach because—oh no—it caused the gurgling to worsen. I placed my hand against my stomach, closed my eyes, and moaned. When I opened them again, Tommy was extending another cup of gooey death toward me.

"No way." I shook my head—another bad idea—and backed away from him and his mystery concoction. "That stuff tastes like the bottom of a compost pile."

"You have to drink two cups for it to work."

"I'll just have a headache, thanks." I kept backing away from him, bumping into displays of merchandise, but he followed, a mischievous look on his face.

The next thing I knew, he was chasing me around the office, determined to get the disgusting goo down my throat.

I dodged and weaved around coolers, T-shirts, and disposable cameras.

"Come on, don't be such a pansy," Tommy said as he drew nearer and almost latched onto my arm.

"You won't take me alive!" I said, laughing as I eluded yet another of his grabs for me.

"You're going down," he said, and lunged again, knocking over the stand of rubber duckies for the upcoming charity river race.

The sight of little yellow rubber ducks flying through the air made me pause long enough for Tommy to catch the sleeve of my T-shirt. I wiggled and pulled to get away, causing Tommy to slip on a duck and fall forward. I barely escaped the flying goo, but he wasn't so lucky.

He lifted himself to his knees and extended his arms to his sides. He now wore his cure-all across the front of his T-shirt and half his face. "You win, love."

I covered my mouth with my hand but couldn't stifle a laugh, then another. "What is it they say, you reap what you sow?"

Tommy rose to his feet and moved very close to me, his green-splattered face only inches from mine. "Remember that, because revenge will be mine."

I laughed again as he headed for the restroom to de-goo himself. Still smiling, I turned to ask Sean why he hadn't come to my rescue. But all I saw of him was his back as he walked out the rear door without a word. No "Hey, I'm heading out to ready the rafts" or anything. My laughs and smile died away.

I walked over to the window and watched him down below, pulling the two necessary rafts out for the first trip of the day, a short morning jaunt for some people staying nearby at a church retreat.

How could someone I'd known my entire life, who had been one of my best friends, be such a mystery to me now? It seemed like everything he did could have multiple meanings. Things would be so much easier if I could just read his mind—that is, if I liked his thoughts.

I leaned closer to the window, watching the way his muscles stretched as he loaded gear. I sighed as I leaned my forehead against the window.

Sean looked up then, as if he sensed me watching him. I jerked away from the window, hoping I'd been quick enough.

Time for some serious thinking and planning. I headed to the storeroom, intent on undertaking said planning while doing mindless work like unpacking stock. Okay, one, I needed to make sure I spent as much time with Sean as possible, both at work and during personal time. Two, I needed to carefully inquire about his months in Denver, what he'd done . . . who he'd hung out with. My heart squeezed when I thought about him out on dates with that other girl, kissing her, maybe even more.

I shook my head, trying to clear the image. Instead, I focused on what Sean and I had had before Dad died and I temporarily lost my mind. I closed my eyes and remembered the kisses we'd shared, a few stolen ones right here in this closet. I smiled when I remembered a particularly nice kiss in here while my grandparents and Mom had only been on the other side of the wall. Sean had smelled like sun-warmed male, having just returned from a rafting trip. He'd grabbed me around the waist and lifted me onto my toes as his mouth had captured mine.

I closed my eyes and relived that kiss. Warm, hungry, enough to make my skin tingle and my fingers dig into Sean's back.

"You smell good."

I yelped at the very in-the-present whisper against my ear.

CHAPTER 8

I spun and tripped over the boxes in the process. I tumbled backward, landing hard on my right hip. And on top of all that, it hadn't even been Sean whispering in my ear.

I stared up at Tommy, who leaned over me with no shirt on and his hair damp from where he'd washed away the goo.

"You startle very easily, boss." He said the word *boss* like he thought it was sexy and he liked teasing me with it.

Okay, I had eyes. Especially sans shirt, the boy was not hard to look at. Tousled hair that was a mixture of blond and auburn, a nice chest as tanned as his arms, trim waist, nice legs.

He reached down to help me up, and I took his hand. He pulled me up faster than I expected, and I found myself standing very close to his unclothed upper half.

"Told you I'd get my revenge," he whispered, so close his breath flowed across my lips.

The enormous flirt thought this was funny, that his being cute and half-clothed would fluster me. "I thought revenge was a bad thing," I said back in as saucy a tone as my relative inexperience could muster.

"Well, this is interesting."

I jerked away from Tommy, managing not to trip and fall on my butt again. Mala stood in the doorway to the storage room, her arms crossed, her eyebrows raised, and many unavoidable questions bubbling below the surface. I imagined her wondering why I was nearly in a clinch with Tommy and if my affections had shifted overnight.

Embarrassed and annoyed that she'd shown up when she had, I mumbled something about Tommy helping me up when I fell as I brushed past her and headed for my desk.

"Without his shirt on?" Mala asked as she followed me. "Last time I checked," she said in a lower voice, "you were still in love with Sean."

"Shh!" I hissed and glanced around her toward the storeroom.

"What?"

I gave her an exasperated look. "Sean and I are friends at most, so give it a rest."

"Look who got up extra pissy this morning."

That she had no clue why I might be "pissy" just added to my foul mood. "Do you ever think before you open your mouth?"

Mala let out a huff. "Is this about me kissing Sean? It was just a stupid game."

"Kiss whoever you want. Just try not to strangle them with your tongue next time."

Mala crossed her arms. "If you and Sean are 'just friends,' you shouldn't be upset. So thanks for being honest with me."

I didn't respond, didn't deny that I was lying. According to Sean, I wasn't very good at it anyway. But I knew my lack of response would annoy Mala, and that was just the kind of mood I was in.

When Tommy emerged from the storage room, pulling a clean Cooley Mountain Whitewater shirt over his head, it didn't appear as if he'd heard anything Mala and I had said. He did, however, wink at me and tap the pitcher of green goo as he passed by the desk and headed outside. Why couldn't we have spilled the entire pitcher instead of just a cup?

Mala pulled a disgusted face at the pitcher, her irritation at me temporarily set aside. "What is this, pureed slime monster?"

I leaned back in my chair, willing to play the "let's avoid the real issue" game. I had to spend the day with my cousin, after all. "That is Tommy's hangover cure-all, and the reason why he wasn't wearing a shirt."

"What, you puked on him?"

"No, I didn't puke on him! He chased me around the office, trying to get me to drink more of that vile mess, and he ended up wearing it."

We both glanced at the front door when it opened. Daniel strolled in and went straight for the day's schedule. He mumbled a "good morning" to us without really looking up and headed for the snack stash. These guys were always hungry. The thought of food right now made me queasy.

"Good to see another chipper person roll in this morning," Mala said.

Daniel met her gaze. "I'm not a morning person. You

should know that by now." He took a drink of his Dr. Pepper, seeking the necessary caffeine to kick-start his day.

"Up too late reading another great work of literature?" she asked as she pointed to the book poking out of the top of his back pocket.

He gave her a challenging look. "You should try it some-time, see if your brain can stretch that far."

Mala huffed. "I read all the time."

"I bet."

Mala narrowed her eyes at him, perturbed that he'd one-upped her again. I nearly laughed, and decided Daniel was my new favorite person for not falling under the Spell of Mala.

Mala turned her back to him and faced me. "If you like Sean," she said low, as if the entire conversation with Daniel hadn't happened, "you've got to do something about it. Be proactive."

I let out a sigh as I rubbed my temples. "It's not that simple."

Mala exhaled in exasperation. "It's not that hard, either." She glanced over at Daniel again. "While we're planning the party, there's no reason we can't all still hang out. Hey, Dan-iel, we're all going to the new drive-in over in Parson tonight. Think you can pull yourself away from Chaucer or Dickens or whoever long enough to go?"

He shrugged as he ambled toward the back door, his hand in a bag of mini chocolate chip cookies. "Sure."

"Don't hurt yourself being so excited," Mala said as the door closed behind Daniel.

"Why do you try to bug him all the time?"

"Because he makes it so easy." She made a flippy motion with her hand. "Not much else to do around here."

"There's plenty of work." I pointed toward the boxes of brochures advertising both Cooley River Whitewater and other area businesses that needed to be placed in the rack near the front door.

"I meant something interesting," she said as she grabbed the box cutter.

"You might have to figure out something else soon, because Daniel seems to be learning how to shoot right back."

Mala snorted. "He got in a couple of easy jabs, one while I was drunk and one before 8 a.m. That hardly makes him champion sparring material."

"Whatever." My pounding head, the bickering with Mala, and my turbulent feelings for Sean made me not want to talk anymore. If only Mala would take the hint and zip it.

Over the next few minutes, she did manage to stay quiet as she restocked the brochure rack. In fact, she seemed lost in her own thoughts. Maybe she was cooking up another attack on Daniel or wondering if her latest issue of *Cosmo* would arrive today. I didn't much care what was going on in her head as long as nothing came out of her mouth.

Even with the quiet, I couldn't concentrate on work. While I was answering an e-mail, my mind would try to sneak off to thoughts of Sean. Despite my annoyance with Mala, the idea of sitting under the stars watching a movie with Sean did have definite appeal. Yet another opportunity to hang out with him and judge how he acted around me. I couldn't help hoping that we'd eventually get back to the point where he might steal kisses in the supply room.

I realized the sound of brochure replenishment had ceased. When I glanced at Mala, she was staring at me with a self-satisfied smile on her face.

"I knew you still liked him. I love it when I'm right." She broke down the boxes for recycling and shoved them behind the storage rack while I sat like a lump, neither affirming nor denying. "I'll pick you up at six thirty." Happy with her triumph, she bounded out the front door to set up the bike rentals for the day.

I tried not to be annoyed by her ability to read me, or by her perkiness, but the task proved impossible. And why was I the only one who appeared to have a hangover? I eyed the green goo and decided I'd rather just suffer.

CHAPTER 9

Thankfully, my hangover and nausea wore off before we left for Parson. Otherwise, Mala's driving on the curvy, mountainous roads would have had me tossing cookies in every direction. And seeing as how we had six people piled into her car, no one would have been safe.

I managed to read the blur of a sign as we passed it— Parson, 3 Miles. When I reached to pull out my movie ticket money, I realized my purse wasn't beside me.

"Crap!"

"What's wrong?" Tommy asked from his spot next to me.

"I forgot my purse." I looked up at Mala, who glanced at me in the rearview mirror. "I told you not to rush me."

"It's okay. We'll pool our money and get you in," Tommy said.

I took a deep breath as Mala rounded another curve. Then I grabbed the back of the seat in front of me as she made an unexpected turn into the parking area for the Grandy Peak Trail.

"I have a better idea," Mala said as she stopped and turned to face me.

I wasn't going to like this, I could tell.

"God, I hope it's a better idea than letting you drive," Chad said, his face an unattractive shade of ghostly.

Mala smacked him on his thick shoulder. "I didn't see you volunteering to drive."

"I drive a truck, genius."

From my perch next to the passenger-side door of the backseat, I asked, "So what's the big idea?"

"If we put two people in the trunk, we can get in for the cheaper, four-max carload rate instead of the individual price. Alex, since you were the one who forgot your purse, you're a given."

"What?" I screeched.

"Oh, come on. Stop being so dramatic. It's not like I'm driving cross-country." Mala looked at Sean. "Be a sport and ride back there with her."

"I'll pay the extra," Sean said.

I couldn't help myself. I looked across Tommy to Sean. Was he trying to be nice, or did he not want to be that close to me? He was, after all, sitting on the opposite side of the car. But then that could have been because Tommy dragged me into the car beside him, leaving Sean with only one option. Sean could have scooted in next to me, putting me in the middle, but maybe he remembered I hated riding in the middle.

Tommy pulled out his wallet. "How much does everyone have?"

When we had a final tally, Mala smiled. "See, not enough to get everyone in and still have enough to eat."

"How much you planning to eat?"

"I didn't have dinner, okay?"

"Fine," I bit out. This deserved one hell of a payback.

Mala blew kisses toward both Sean and me. "Have fun back there. We'll let you out once we're inside."

"You don't think someone's going to see them climbing out of the trunk?" Tommy asked.

"Not if I park at the very back," Mala replied.

Sean and I exited our respective sides of the car and headed toward the trunk that popped open as we reached it. We exchanged a wary glance and waited as two cars drove by. Then Sean jumped in and scooted as far back as possible, leaving me as much space as he could.

My heart thudded like crazy. Wow, the trunk looked way smaller with Sean taking up so much of it. As I stared at what little carpeted real estate was left, I was faced with another conundrum. Did I crawl in facing him or with my back to him? Either way, it was going to be close quarters. Mala's idea of getting us together, literally, no doubt.

Mala got out of the car and came back to stand next to me, but with her face out of sight of Sean. She grinned wide and winked at me. "What are you waiting for, the polar ice caps to melt?"

I gave her a stare that promised retribution. She did that fake shaking-in-her-boots shimmy. Betting that I'd feel marginally less claustrophobic if I faced outward, I hopped into the trunk with Sean.

Mala stepped to the back of the car and smiled down at us. "Don't do anything I wouldn't do."

I heard Daniel say, "That leaves it wide open," before Mala shut the trunk and plunged us into darkness. I stiffened against the immediate feeling of being trapped, buried.

Sean rested his hand on my shoulder and squeezed gently. "It'll be okay. We're only a couple of miles from the drive-in." His breath was warm against my neck. In any other situation, I'd have loved lying this close to him. As it stood, I was trapped in a car trunk with someone who shouldn't even have been nice to me, after what I'd done. Why wasn't it as easy to right wrongs as it was to commit them?

Gravel crunched as the car started to move. When we returned to the road, the floor of the trunk vibrated. I noticed a rubbery smell, whether from the tires on the car or the spare that was stored below us, I didn't know. Then I thought I smelled exhaust fumes, and my heart rate kicked up even more.

"I swear, if I asphyxiate back here, I'm so going to come back and haunt Mala for the rest of her life. And believe me, I'll appear at the most inopportune moments."

Sean laughed. "She'd deserve it, but we won't asphyxiate. This is a newer car. It has an emergency release handle inside here." He guided my hand to it to reassure me.

"Good to know," I said, relaxing a little. Well, the part of me nervous about being in the trunk of a moving car relaxed. The part that was jittery about being pressed close to the guy I wanted so much I couldn't stand it sometimes? Not so much.

"Really, this isn't so bad," he said. "A few more minutes and we'll be inside the drive-in. And maybe Mala will have had her fun and the rest of the night will be free of her craziness."

"True. Guess there's an upside to everything."

"Yeah, there is." His words came out so low I almost didn't hear them over the car's engine. Had he meant for me to hear them? If I'd been Mala, I'd have been scooting back against Sean, using the situation for all it was worth. But I wasn't Mala. And before I started using what little feminine wiles I possessed, I had a huge apology to make. I had planned to wait until I found just the right time and place, the right words, was sure he'd be receptive to those words, but . . . what the hell?

"Sean, I—" Before I could utter anything more, the car turned sharply and I slid, banging my head against the side of the trunk. "Ow!"

"You okay?"

"I'm so going to put Nair in her shampoo bottle."

Gravel pinged against the underside of the car, making conversation impossible. Maybe it was a sign this wasn't the right time to get into what would likely to be a long, uncomfortable conversation anyway.

When Mala braked again, I slid backward into Sean. He wrapped his arm around me, which caused me to hold my breath. Oh, this felt so good. His arm holding me close, his body heat soaking into me, the hardness of his chest against my back.

"I think your cousin is bordering on loony."

I let my breath out slowly, trying not to sound like my

hormones were revving like a race car's engine. "You're not telling me anything I don't know."

One second, I was lying snuggled close to Sean. The next, someone jerked open the trunk and shone a bright flashlight in our faces. I lifted my hand to block the light, and I felt Sean duck his head behind me to shield his own eyes.

"Okay, out," said a male voice that belonged to someone behind the flashlight.

Crap. Trunk check. Mala didn't know it yet, but her ass was so toast.

I stumbled from the trunk, followed by Sean. The drivers of a couple of cars behind us in line honked. I glanced up and was horrified to see a minivan driven by Mr. Carmichael, our vice principal, directly behind Mala's car.

"I'm going to kill Mala," I said as I hurried around to the side of the car.

Sean and I slid into our former spots in the backseat. I sank low, as if I could make Mr. Carmichael forget he'd seen me. I crossed my arms and stared out the window, irked that I'd let Mala talk me into the trunk trick.

"You need to turn around and leave," the geeky boy running the ticket booth said to Mala.

"Oh, come on. We were just having some fun. We'll pay."

"People caught trying to sneak in are to be turned around."

Mala leaned out her open window and, I swear, batted her eyelashes at the guy. "What if I give you a big tip?"

Geek Boy swallowed hard. "What kind of tip?"

"Get a new wardrobe," Tommy whispered next to me.

I ignored him, focusing instead on the attendant, already knowing he would be mesmerized by Mala's beauty and let us in. It annoyed me when she used her looks to get what she wanted.

"I'm having a party soon. What if I invited you?" Mala gave him her sweet smile.

More honking from further back in the line was accompanied by someone yelling, "Come on, get moving!" Would the earth just crack open and swallow me whole now, please?

"It's going to be a great party," Mala said. "Lots of dancing. And no parents."

The guy looked like he'd taken a not so healthy jolt from a stun gun as he accepted our money and waved us through. Mala, Tommy, and Chad hooted with laughter as she pulled away from the ticket booth and into the drive-in. They might have thought this whole episode was funny, but I was far from amused. I'd nearly started an important conversation with Sean while in the trunk of a car! When all he'd indicated was that we might be friends again.

And then I'd gotten caught trying to sneak in, and had had to crawl out of the trunk none too gracefully while simultaneously ruining my vice principal's impression of me.

When Mala parked in the back row and turned off the car, she was still laughing. "Did you see his face? Ohmygod, this was too funny."

"Yeah, a real riot," I said as I opened the door and stomped out.

Mala came after me. "What's up with you?"

I spun back toward her. "I'm tired of getting sucked into your wild schemes. They never go as planned."

"Jeez, get a grip. We got in, didn't we?"

I pointed back toward the ticket book. "Did you happen to see who was behind us? Mr. Carmichael. I wouldn't be surprised if he was calling Grandma and Grandpa right now."

"He's a dip, but I doubt he's that much of a tattle. It's not like we're breaking some school rule."

I exhaled loudly in frustration.

"Seriously, you're overreacting," Mala said. "It was funny, admit it."

"I don't call getting stuffed in a car trunk, banging my head, and being made to crawl out in front of half the county funny. After the day I've had, getting in trouble would just be the perfect cap."

"Honestly, you have such a stick up your butt sometimes. And I *don't* get you in trouble. You *never* get in trouble." She said the last as if it highly annoyed her.

Let's add memory lapses to wildness and being a tease to my cousin's list of faults. I noticed the people in the cars around us staring. Before I made more of a spectacle of myself, I headed for the concession stand. I felt a bout of emotional eating coming on.

I ordered a hot dog, loaded, plus some nachos, a bag of M&M's, and the largest Coke they had. Then I remembered that my lack of money was what caused the whole trunk fiasco in the first place.

"I got it," Tommy said as he stepped up beside me and pulled several bills from his wallet.

"I thought there wasn't enough money for tickets and food."

"I didn't pay for your ticket, so I have plenty left for snacks." He pointed toward my array of carbs and sugar, then cracked a smile. "Good thing, too."

Suddenly embarrassed by my gluttony, I couldn't meet his eyes as I walked out beside him.

"Thanks."

"No problem. I hear I can get brownie points with the boss this way."

I lifted my snacks. "I tend to eat when I'm upset. It's a wonder I'm not the size of Denver by now."

"You're a long way from that."

"That's sweet of you to say, but you might wait to reserve judgment until *after* I've scarfed all this."

Tommy shot me a mischievous smile. "I solemnly swear to tell you if you suddenly balloon into an enormous elephant."

"Ha ha." It was nice to have a friend who was pure fun and who wasn't all wrapped up in my past. Tommy might tease me a lot, but he had a kind, supportive side as well.

We made our way back toward the others at a much slower pace than I'd escaped them.

"Don't let Mala get to you so much," he said.

"Easy for you to say. You haven't grown up with her."

"She's not all bad."

I let out a sigh. "I know. Sometimes I just wish she'd think more and act impulsive less." That she'd actually care that we'd gotten caught trying to sneak in and I'd nearly died of embarrassment.

"Sometimes impulsive is what we need."

I paused and let him get a couple of steps in front of me. He was right. Mala and her goofball personality had helped get me through the darkest months of my life. I needed to chill, forget about the trunk incident, and enjoy the night. Focus on the fact that Sean didn't seem to hate me and figure out exactly what his feelings were.

When we reached our friends, they were all sitting on blankets outside the car. It dawned on me that Mala had been the one to pay my entry price, so I extended my nachos toward her as a peace offering. After a moment's hesitation, she took a couple. As we talked and watched the previews, I caught Sean watching me a few times. What was he thinking? About how close we'd been in the trunk? Had he put his arm around me to protect me or himself in the bouncing car? Or had he just wanted to? Was that a move toward getting back together, or wishful thinking on my part? Why, oh why, couldn't I be a mind reader?

Oh, and I found it supremely annoying that guys evidently didn't torture themselves this way.

The awareness between us, at least on my part, caused the nerves in my stomach to start roiling. So much for eating my scads of food.

Part of me wanted to be alone with him, to get everything out in the open. But I was scared, too, and glad for the safety in numbers.

Tommy interrupted my stream of thoughts by leaning

across me to nab some of my nachos. I smelled alcohol and realized he must have snuck something in and added it to his Coke.

"I might as well take these off your hands since you're not eating them."

Desperate to lighten the mood—at least *my* mood—I tossed a chip at him. "Food thievery something you Brits commit often?"

"Only from pretty colonial girls," he said and bumped my nose with a cheese-covered chip.

"Eew!" I grabbed a napkin and wiped away the cheese, then wadded up the napkin and pitched it at Tommy.

He responded by throwing popcorn at me. "Be careful. You don't want to start an international incident."

"Are you picking on my cousin?" Mala asked, and stuffed a piece of popcorn in Tommy's ear.

In the next moment food was flying everywhere. I dodged more cheese-covered nachos only to have ice dropped down the back of my shirt by Chad. In turn, I squirted a package of ketchup at him, missing horribly but breaking off his assault.

By the time the people in the nearby cars started shushing us, I had nacho cheese in my hair and popcorn down my bra. We kept snickering despite the dirty looks of the other movie watchers.

I hadn't laughed that much since before Dad's death, and it felt good. And the wide smile on Sean's face was the yummy icing on the cake. I was determined to start over, and as more than friends. Maybe we were just circling each other like two cats waiting for the other to make the first real move. That move should go to me, and I would make it. Just not in this group setting. The time and place had to be right. And it was quite possible there would need to be some Pepto-Bismol involved.

At least tonight I felt hopeful.

Our antics drew the attention of some of our classmates. Mari Russell, Amy Leon, and Lily Byrd came over and sat on a corner of the blankets near Chad and Daniel. Mari and Amy went for the jock types, so their attention was focused on Chad. Lily was smart as well as pretty in a very wholesome way, so she and Daniel fell into conversation. They weren't zeroing in on Sean, so the more the merrier, right?

Not according to the look on Mala's face. Even without the benefit of full lighting, I noticed her glare. Mala liked being the center of attention, and the arrival of the other three girls had diverted at least some of that attention away.

"Who did you all come with?" she asked them.

"Just us," Lily said. "Girls' night out."

"The dating pool is pretty slim around here, isn't it?"

Lily's expression cooled as she met Mala's gaze. "Not all of us need a guy to have a good time."

Mala eyed Daniel and Chad, who were flanked by the trio and didn't seem to mind. "Obviously."

I'd swear the next couple of minutes felt like the Olympics of flirting. Mari and Amy were more obvious than Lily in their efforts, but they all paled by comparison to Mala. She scooted closer to Tommy and started feeding him popcorn and laughing a little too loudly at whatever he said.

Tommy wasn't blind, though. He glanced at me and rolled his eyes, which made me nearly snort soda out my nose.

If I hadn't known better, I'd have sworn Mala was drunk again. Maybe there was a little extra something in her soda too. She took flirting to the next level when she slid onto Tommy's lap.

"Jeez, Mala, why don't you just strip down and go at it?" Daniel asked.

My mouth fell open. Once again, Daniel had surprised me. He really had a low tolerance for Mala's antics, but this summer he seemed to be more willing to vocalize it.

Mala didn't miss a step. "Now you seem to be the one wanting to see me naked. We keep having this type of conversation and we're going to have to do something about it."

"Now *that* would get us kicked out," Sean said.

While some of the group laughed, me included, Mala didn't. She slid off Tommy's lap. "Don't worry. I haven't gotten that desperate yet."

Mala stood, and when she turned away from the group, the self-confident look on her face disappeared. When she started walking toward the restrooms at the back of the concession stand building, I got to my feet and followed her.

"Mala?"

She held up her hand. "Save it if you're going to tell me what a big ho I am too."

I grabbed her arm and forced her to stop. "Jump to conclusions much? I wasn't going to say that."

"After the past twenty-four hours, you can understand why I'd think that."

"What's with you? When have you ever cared what anyone else said about you?"

She stared at me a moment too long before saying, "I
don't. I just had to pee." Mala resumed walking toward the
restroom. I followed, wondering about that too-long pause.
Maybe Mala wasn't as thick-skinned as I'd always believed.

"You know you bring it on yourself, right?"

"If you're here to lecture me about propriety, you can just
leave."

"I'm not lecturing. But why are you surprised when people react to how you behave?"

Mala stopped again just outside the restroom door and
glanced back toward our friends. "I'm not surprised. I set
myself up for it, right?"

"Then why are you upset?"

"I'm not."

I shook my head. "And you accused me of lying."

"I'm fine, so stop making up weird scenarios in your head."
She made a shooing motion with her hand. "Go hang out with
Sean before one of the Ta-Ta Trio decides he's fair game."

"Mala—"

"Damn, Alex, I'm about to wet myself here. I'll be back
in a few. I've got to buy another Coke, too. Tommy knocked
mine over during the melee."

I threw up my hands in surrender. "Fine." See if I tried
to be supportive again. I wasn't going to pry the truth out of
her, whatever it was.

When I returned to the group, I sat next to Sean, mind-
ful of what Mala had said about the other girls.

He leaned over and asked, "What's wrong with Mala?"

"She's just getting another Coke."

I kept my eyes lowered so he didn't check for the wide-eyed giveaway that I was lying. Well, I wasn't really, just not divulging the whole truth.

"Was she mad?"

I shrugged. "You know Mala. Nothing much bothers her." The words didn't sound true in my mouth anymore.

The sound of a motorcycle startled everyone. We all looked toward the noise in time to see Mala ride up on the back of D. J. Forrester's bike. D. J. was likely harmless, but he gave off that wrong-side-of-the-tracks bad-boy vibe anyway. Our class would probably have voted him Most Likely to End Up in a Cover Band. He stopped in front of us long enough for Mala to toss her car keys at me and say, "Later!" with a wave. Then D. J. gunned the motorcycle, and they roared off, neither wearing helmets, drowning out the sound of the movie.

So much for her caring what everyone thought of her. I sighed and looked back toward the group. My friends were already back to their interrupted conversations. Everyone but Daniel. He watched Mala ride away with D. J., a very tight look on his face. Everyone knew he thought Mala was a flake, but what I couldn't figure out was why he let her irritate him so much. She fed on that, and she'd likely have stopped if he'd simply ignored her.

A bit of conversation dragged my attention away from Daniel.

"They'll be here tomorrow," Sean said.

"Who?" I asked.

"My friends from Denver. They're coming up to stay for a few days."

His friends from Denver? The people he'd spent the past nine months with during his first school year away from Golden Bend. People who were not me. Was the mystery girl among them? Was she prettier and more sophisticated than me? More fun? I hated his parents' divorce even more than before. If they'd stayed together, he would have remained here in Golden Bend. Maybe we could have repaired our relationship by now. And he wouldn't have even met that other girl.

Oh God, what if she was still his girlfriend? And she was coming here tomorrow. That didn't leave me any time to find out if Sean could be convinced we should be more than friends, to have our long-overdue conversation. Unless I instigated it tonight.

I swallowed hard and lost my appetite all over again.

CHAPTER 10

The combination of lack of opportunity and an acute attack of the nerves on my part had prevented any big revelations to Sean the previous night. The nerves were still my constant companions this morning. I kept going back and forth about what I should do. I could risk mortification if I admitted my true feelings only to find out Sean had a girlfriend. Or I could keep my mouth closed and suffer in silence when she breezed in and ripped the last of my hope away. Wow, what a fabulous choice.

I was stocking gift shop shelves with Cooley Mountain Whitewater hats when three guys close to my age came in. My attention was immediately drawn to the first guy in the door. Why? Because he had red hair in dreadlocks. He reminded me of Olympic snowboarder Shaun White, just more Rastafarian.

"Hey," he said, then offered me a friendly smile.

Red hair with dreads doesn't sound attractive, but he was actually pretty cute.

"Interested in rafting?" I asked as I descended the stepladder.

"Maybe later. We're looking for Sean Kenley."

My breath caught. "Oh, you must be his friends from Denver." And they were early. At least there were no girls among them.

"Yes, and our boy has been holding out. He didn't tell us about the beautiful women up here."

I blushed. It'd been a long time since anyone had flirted with me. Well, other than Tommy, but he flirted with every female within a ten-mile radius.

"Sorry, no free rafting trips in exchange for compliments," I said.

He smiled again, wider, more mischievous this time. "That's not what the flyer said."

The front door opened again, drawing away Dread Guy's attention. Sean walked in, and much shoulder bumping and backslapping ensued. Guys being guys. Forgotten for the moment, I stood to the side and watched them. Envied their closeness with Sean.

Sean caught my eye first. "Guys, this is Alex. Her family owns the place."

"The beauty has a name," Dread Guy said, causing a flicker of something that looked suspiciously like annoyance in Sean's eyes for a moment.

"Alex, this is Ian," Sean said, indicating Dread Guy, "Austin, and Kirk."

I nodded and uttered an unremarkable "hey" to them, then went back to my halfhearted work. I listened to Sean and his friends talk about their respective summers so far and gossip about a bunch of people I didn't know in Denver.

People from that unknown part of Sean's life. It felt like part of my memory had been erased, only it had never been there to begin with.

"So, who else is headed up?" Sean asked his friends.

Ian gave me a wink before redirecting his attention to Sean. "Jamie, if he can get away from his warden of a mother. Nicole and Ashlee."

Crap. Girls. Which one was *the* girl? I imagined someone named Nicole or Ashlee on Sean's arm, going out to dinner with him, snuggling close to him during a movie, kissing him. I knocked a stack of hats off the end of the shelf, and they took down a display of bagged popcorn in the process.

"She's cute *and* clumsy," Ian said as he bent to retrieve the scattered hats. When he looked up at me and smiled, I found it difficult to muster a smile back with all those images of another girl pawing Sean in my head.

"Thanks," I said as he handed me the hats. When his hand touched mine, I noticed he had nice, strong, tanned hands. I also became aware that he was giving me an interested perusal, and my skin warmed in response.

"What's the plan?" Sean asked, drawing away Ian's attention.

"We're headed out to Lake Whittaker this afternoon, use my dad's boat," said Kirk, who reminded me of Zac Efron, with his emo haircut. His clothing looked like it had arrived from the Lands' End catalog yesterday.

I wondered if Ashlee and Nicole would be similarly attired, or would they wear some chic clothes from a Denver boutique? I looked down at my own khaki shorts and dark blue Cooley Mountain Whitewater polo. I wasn't exactly Heidi Klum, was I? I fought the desperate need to go shopping for something cute and eye-catching.

Tommy and Chad wandered in the back door, done with their first rafting trip of the day.

"You should invite your friends along this afternoon," Ian said. "We'll head out after you close up shop." He redirected his eyes to me. "I like a good sunset cruise."

Wow, I thought, Tommy had better watch out, or he might lose the flirting crown now that Ian had rolled into town.

"Where we going?" Tommy asked, always ready for an adventure or party. He was milking this "American experience" for every last iota of fun.

"Out on Lake Whittaker," Sean answered. Did he sound less enthusiastic than he had a minute ago?

"Great idea, lads. I'm in."

Ian looked at me. "What about you?"

Lake Whittaker was huge compared to the river, but it was calm and had no rapids or dangerous turns. I paused long enough that Sean caught my eye. I couldn't tell what he was thinking, what he hoped I'd say.

"You should go," he finally said. "And Mala and the rest of the guys."

"Sounds good." I'd deal with my reaction to the water when the time came. I couldn't stand the thought of sitting at home while some sexy girl from Denver had him to herself. If they were still a couple, it'd be painful to witness. But would it be worse than staying away and not knowing? If this girl was the reason Sean wanted to be just friends with me, I needed to see her with my own eyes.

And perhaps I'd devise a plan to make Sean see that it was really me he wanted.

Mala and I were the last ones to the boat dock, since we had to close the office and our last rafters of the day wanted to come in after their trip to book some more visits. With all the gang from Cooley Mountain plus the Denver crew, there were a total of eleven of us.

As we stood on the dock, Sean made more introductions. As I'd feared, Ashlee and Nicole were both stunningly gorgeous. Nicole had chocolate-colored hair to her shoulders and exotic-looking dark eyes. Ashlee's long, straight, black hair and dark eyes made her look like a modern-day Cleopatra.

As if my gut instinct to dislike her wasn't bad enough, Ashlee laced her fingers through Sean's as she smiled wide at me, showing me—what else?—perfect teeth. My heart contracted painfully, and I had to look away for several seconds to get my surging hurt and anger under control. I imagined my claws lengthening when I looked at her again. All I saw was the word *ENEMY* in big, fat letters across her forehead.

Almost as soon as we boarded the pontoon, Kirk headed his dad's boat out across the lake. I quelled my nervousness by doing some deep breathing that probably made me look like someone leading a yoga class. But, hey, being nervous about drowning tended to take the edge off seeing another girl holding the hand of the guy your heart belonged to.

I tried to focus on the fact that the hand-holding didn't last long and that Sean talked to everyone aboard the *USS Hormone* almost equally. Still, I found myself wishing I'd never seen them together and that the trip was over. I mean, what could I do other than talk to Sean in a casual sort of way? I couldn't reveal my feelings now, when he'd given no indication he felt more for me than tentative friendship, when there was no means of escape if he shot me down. I didn't particularly fancy humiliating myself or swimming back to shore.

Plus, even if there wasn't anything between them now, I could tell Sean and Ashlee had been involved at some point and that Ashlee wanted to pick up where they'd left off. Lot of that going around.

I wasn't the only one irked by the current situation. Daniel had been engrossed in conversation with Nicole—turned out she was a burgeoning writer as well as beautiful—almost from the moment we boarded the boat. Mala had tried to join in the conversation a couple of times, but that had worked about as well as a campfire in the rain.

About as well as me pretending to be cool with seeing Sean and Ashlee so close.

But while I grew nauseous and escaped to the rail in case I puked, Mala started hanging all over Austin. In fact, as I looked back over my shoulder, I noticed they'd moved from outrageous flirting to kissing.

"Your cousin appears to be the take-charge kind of gal," Ian said as he walked up next to me and leaned backward on the rail I faced.

"Yep."

"What about you?"

I shrugged. "Depends."

"On?"

I turned halfway toward Ian. I focused all my attention on him—partly to escape the awkwardness of watching Sean with Ashlee and, quite frankly, partly because Ian wasn't too difficult to look at.

"On if there's anything worth taking charge of."

Ian raised his eyebrows, and a sense of empowerment I'd not felt in ages surged through me.

"A woman who knows what she wants. I like it." He spun around to face the water, then pointed at a wooded island. "We're going to pull up there so we can build a fire and have a cookout."

The sound of Ashlee laughing behind me made me cringe despite my momentary reprieve with Ian.

Our arrival at the island couldn't come fast enough. I could escape Ashlee's obvious displays of affection, including the touches to Sean's arm and the laughter that made me cringe. I could run into the woods and hide, since that seemed to be my MO when around Sean and girls who were throwing themselves at him. I wondered if I could just live out there on the island and have Mala bring me food every few days. I could even name the place Pathetic Loser Island.

"Great," I said after a long pause.

Ian eyed me. "You okay?"

I glanced over at him and realized I was being too obvious and, well, pathetic. I didn't want to be mopey girl, even though that was how I felt inside, like I'd blown my one chance and the current situation was my fault. Still sucked.

I took a deep breath and focused on Ian.

"Yeah. This is fun. I'm so used to the river that it's nice to come out on the lake." Actually, that wasn't a total lie. Part of me missed being out on the river every day, the part that had forgotten how deadly it was and how wildly my heart beat every time I considered it. But the lake was a nice middle ground, so to speak, between the rapids and constant dry land. There were no whirlpools or strong currents here to take me under.

When Kirk maneuvered the boat next to the island and I jumped down to the thin slice of sandy beach, Ian took my hand.

"This will be fun," Ashlee said as she walked alongside Sean onto the beach. "Like when we all went skiing."

"Hopefully you won't try to wrap yourself around a tree this time," Sean said.

Ashlee swatted his arm. "It was a bush, not a tree. Quit exaggerating."

Sean laughed as he dodged another swat.

Agreeing to go on this outing had to have been my worst decision ever.

Ian's hand squeezed mine. "We're going to gather some firewood," he said to the others, and led me to the wooded area beyond the beach.

His hand felt warm but not sweaty against mine, reassuring in an odd way. I entwined my fingers more securely with his.

I glanced back at Sean and saw Ashlee doing her best to become his shadow, smiling wide and giggling as she did it. Anger bubbled up in me like oil from a well. I averted my gaze and allowed Ian to lead the way. I knew he had more on his mind than gathering firewood, but I didn't care. A girl could only handle so much before she exploded, right? After all, Sean wasn't making a move in my direction, and Ian was. I deserved a little fun of my own.

Once we were out of sight of the others, Ian stopped and pulled me closer to him. This felt weird, being held in another guy's arms, but not entirely bad.

"Finally, I have you all to myself," he said, his voice deepening and his fingertips trailing down the side of my face.

"And just what do you think you're going to do with me?" I asked, sounding like I was channeling Mala.

"This." My eyelids drifted closed as his head lowered toward mine. When his lips touched mine, I tilted my head and kissed him back. The next thing I knew, he'd backed me against a tree trunk and deepened the kiss. A shot of adrenaline made me respond with enthusiasm.

I wove my fingers through his dreads. They felt funny yet familiar, like the rigging on our rafts. His hands made their way down my back. My heart rate increased. I wondered if maybe Ian could help me forget Sean. He smelled like some woodsy cologne mixed with the ever-present Colorado pines.

Eventually, the knowing hooting from the beach caused us to break apart. With some snickering of our own, we gathered firewood and headed back. When we exited the woods onto the beach, clapping and more hooting greeted us. While I lowered my head to hide my red face, Ian looked proud of himself and actually took a bow. Typical guy.

Try as I might, I couldn't keep from glancing toward Sean. He was staring at me with a strange look on his face. In the fading light I couldn't tell if it was jealousy, disappointment, or disgust—or all three. I lowered my eyes. But as I dropped the firewood next to the fire pit the others had created, I got mad. What did he expect from me anyway? Especially when Miss Glamour Pants was virtually attached to him, breathing the same air?

I ignored Sean as we coaxed a fire into existence, then roasted hot dogs. I tried to play mind games with myself, pretending I didn't know anyone named Sean, that he wasn't sitting across the fire from me, that I didn't want to be sitting where Ashlee had perched.

No surprise here—it didn't work.

Ian didn't make any hint of another move, but that didn't bother me. I couldn't manage to care if it was because I was a sucky kisser or because he had satisfied his curiosity and was moving on. I guessed he was Mr. Live in the Moment. I wondered if I should adopt that policy.

But while the extent of my and Ian's "relationship" had come and gone, Mala and Austin were still going strong. Another infatuation, another flavor of the month. I actually envied her. Not because she was playing sucky-face with Austin, but because she didn't allow herself to get so wrapped up in someone that trying to break free of those feelings was like trying to escape a strong undertow. I wondered why we were so different in that respect.

Granted, I'd made out with Ian, but I wondered if Mala and Austin were doing a bit more than that when the rest of us were getting ready to leave and found that the two of them had disappeared from the area around the fire. But instead of yelling for them, the Denver crew thought it'd be funny to leave Austin and Mala on the island.

"You can't leave Mala out here," I said.

"You know she'd do it to you," Chad said.

"Remember the car trunk," Tommy added.

They were right, but still. While I might envy Mala's carefree outlook, did I *really* want to act like her?

"It's only for a little while," Ian assured me as he lightly bumped my shoulder with his. "Just long enough to scare them. Come on, it'll be hilarious."

I glanced at Sean to see what he thought, but he was too busy talking to Ashlee to even register an opinion.

I noticed Daniel eyeballing the dark woods. I thought he was about to object to the plan too. Despite how much Mala annoyed him, I couldn't imagine he thought this was the right thing to do. Instead of saying so, however, he turned away and walked toward the boat.

Vastly outnumbered, I agreed to the practical joke and climbed on board. Back on the water, my anxiety returned, but this time part of it had to do with leaving Mala behind. Yes, I'd joked about taking up solo residence on the island, but in reality I would have likely freaked out.

On the positive side, this did pay Mala back for the car trunk incident. Revenge was kind of sweet.

I sat back, closed my eyes, and breathed deeply of the cool night air as we moved across the lake.

The beep of my phone startled me. I pulled it from my pocket and saw Mala's cell number on the display. When I saw the text, my heart sank.

All it said was "911."

CHAPTER 11

When I tried to call Mala, I got no answer. Oh my God, what had happened? Why had I left her there, and with a guy she didn't really know? What if Austin had done something to her?

"Turn the boat around!"

"We're not that far away from the island. They've barely even had time to notice we're gone," Ashlee said.

I squeezed my phone until the hard plastic dug into my skin. I forced myself to look away from Ashlee and stared at Kirk. "Turn around, now."

"What's wrong?" Sean asked as he took a step toward me. Even though I'd barely been able to look at him all afternoon, now I was glad someone who knew when I wasn't joking was here. "Mala texted me a 911 message, and now I can't get her on the phone."

"She's probably just trying to get us to come back," Chad said.

"No. We've always agreed that we'd only text that if we were really in trouble and needed help."

"Get back to the island," Daniel said to Kirk.

Though I appreciated his help, it ticked me off that Kirk listened to him and not me. How could Sean be friends with these people?

I clung to the metal railing around the edge of the boat as Kirk pushed the pontoon to its upper speed limit, which might have been ten miles per hour considering how loaded it was. I wished we'd taken out some type of boat that moved faster.

"She'll be okay," Sean said from beside me. He reached over and squeezed my hand for a brief moment.

I hoped he was right, but I didn't think even Mala would play with the 911 message. I imagined all sorts of horrible things, as it seemed to take forever to return to the island. When we came within sight of the beach, my anxiety shot sky-high. Mala was sitting on the sand with her head between her knees. Austin stood close to her.

Mala struggled to her feet as Kirk nearly beached the boat but pulled back on the throttle in time. "Where were you?" she screamed as I jumped in at the very edge of the water and slogged my way toward her.

"I'm sorry. Are you hurt?"

Half hysterical, Mala held out her hand. "I was bitten by a snake!"

"It was just a green snake, harmless," Austin said. "But she won't listen."

Mala spun on him. "You weren't the one bitten, so shut up!"

I grabbed the upper part of Mala's arms and shook her. "Calm down. Did you see it? Was it a green snake?"

"Maybe."

Austin let out an exasperated sound and sloshed through the water to the boat.

"Okay, yeah, it was green."

I felt like all strength was flowing out of me. "It was a green snake. Mala, you've lived here your entire life. You know they're not dangerous. Why did you nine-one-one me?" My voice rose with each question, anger replacing worry.

"I freaked, okay? Plus, you left me behind."

I clenched my jaw as I stared at her, trying to get my anger under control. "Why didn't you answer when I called you back?"

"I dropped my phone in the water. It didn't work when I fished it out."

I closed my eyes, did my best to breathe evenly, and ran my hands back over my hair. My cousin was going to be the death of me yet. "Just get in the boat."

She didn't argue. By the time I turned around, some of the guys were helping her onboard. I followed and allowed Sean and Chad to pull me up as well.

"Got bit by a snake, huh?" Ashlee asked while shifting her gaze between Mala and Austin and trying to stifle a laugh. Others on the boat didn't even try to hide theirs.

"Yes, she was," I said in hard, clipped words. I gave her my best evil-bitch stare. "And a real one, not what your overly amorous friend carries around in his pants."

Everyone froze for a moment at my icy tone. Okay, so that response had way more to do with my feelings toward

Ashlee than Austin, but whatever. It got my point across. "Get this friggin' boat back to the dock."

Kirk didn't question me this time as he backed away from the island and set us on a course for shore.

Spent, I sank down onto the bench next to Mala.

"Thanks—"

I held up my hand, halting whatever she'd been about to say. "You don't want to hear anything I might say right now."

It was very un-Mala-like, but she stayed quiet. To our complete and utter surprise, Daniel sat down on the other side of Mala. He took her hand in his and examined the bite. It took me a moment to remember that Daniel had more first-aid training than the rest of us. Taking care of someone who was hurt would override even how much Mala drove him insane.

"Most likely a harmless bite, but we'll take you to the hospital just to be sure," he said.

His words seemed to calm Mala some, though I could tell she was going to be in freak-out mode until an actual doctor told her she wasn't going to die or that her arm wasn't going to rot with poison and fall off.

Though Kirk threw the throttle wide open, it still seemed to take forever to cross back over the lake. My blowup had stifled conversation, and I imagined a giant wedge driven between Mala and me. Even though I was trying to ignore her, I noticed that she kept scratching the lower part of her back. When I glanced over, I spotted a rash on the skin between her shorts and her short tee. Green snakes weren't poisonous, but maybe Mala was having an allergic reaction to the bite. So why was it on her back while the bite area only looked a little red?

Whatever was going on, I wasn't about to point it out to Mala. Of course, as I thought this, she reached back to scratch the splotchy area again. Out of instinct, I grabbed her hand to keep her from doing so.

"Let go. I've got an itch."

"Um, that might not be a good idea."

"Why not?"

"You . . ." Oh, crap, I had to tell her now. I lowered my voice. "You've got a rash."

"A rash," she said as if I'd told her she had some deadly disease. "Oh God, I'm dying." She dropped her face to her upturned hands.

That was when I noticed the leaves and twigs in her hair. Well, no mystery how she'd gotten the rash and the forest-floor hair accessories. Rolling around on the ground with a guy tended to have those kinds of consequences. Thank goodness I'd done my impromptu making out standing up.

"Daniel, can you get Mala some water?"

"Sure," he said, then headed to the cooler.

"You might want to get the twigs and leaves out of your hair," I said when he'd moved away.

Mala reached up and pulled the incriminating evidence out of her hair and tossed it overboard.

"You can relax about the rash. I don't think it has anything to do with the bite."

She lifted her face to look at me. A look of comprehension crossed her features, quickly followed by a flush that camouflaged her currently blotchy complexion. Then she turned her attention to Austin. "I'm going to kill him. I told him I didn't want to lie down in the middle of the freakin' woods."

I let out a sigh. "Then why did you?"

I feared she might fly off into a tirade. Instead, she leaned back and crossed her arms. "My taste in guys totally sucks pond water."

I couldn't argue with her there. Sure, I'd made mistakes, some big ones. But Mala tended to make mistakes more often, and typically of the variety that involved acting before thinking.

Kirk finally pulled up to the dock.

I steered Mala off the boat and toward my Jeep. The sooner we got this over with, the sooner I could go home and fall into bed and dream about pushing needles into a voodoo doll that looked like Ashlee.

When we reached the hospital several minutes later, I began to actually worry about Mala. She looked like she might vomit at any moment and would have given Kermit a run for his money in the green department. I wasn't sure how much of this was actual physical reaction to the bite and rash and how much would prove psychological.

A nurse guided Mala toward an examining room while I stayed behind to deal with the paperwork and, oh joy of joys, call her parents. My aunt sighed in exasperation instead of sounding scared. Her reaction struck me as sort of sad. I couldn't imagine my mom reacting that way. But then, I never gave her reason to.

When I finished my thrilling tasks, I headed to the waiting room and found Sean, Tommy, Chad, and Daniel there. The conspicuous absence of the Denverites, especially Austin, reignited my anger.

"Where are your *friends*?"

Sean looked up, startled by the accusatory tone of my question. "I told them to go on back to their hotel."

I wanted to say something smart-ass and snarky, but I couldn't come up with anything. Truthfully, I was glad the Denverites weren't there. If they had been, I might have punched Austin for being such a horndog and spit on Ashlee for daring to touch Sean. That wouldn't have made me too appealing to Sean, would it? And despite everything, I still cared about him. Even if *he* still liked Ashlee. What guy wouldn't like such a hot girl hanging all over him like cling wrap?

Plus, there was that genuine look of concern in his hypnotic eyes when he asked, "How's Mala?"

"They haven't told me yet, but I'm guessing she'll live to flirt another day." I sank into a chair and tried not to look at Sean or acknowledge the weird quiet amongst our group.

I mean, what were they going to ask beyond, "How's Mala?" I couldn't imagine any of them suddenly blurting out, "So, was Mala really out in the woods banging a guy she'd just met?"

I wanted to scream, "Do over!" and begin this day anew. I'd catch Sean before work and finally admit how I felt. If he felt the same, fabulous! If not, I would totally skip the boating excursion and trying to replace him in my heart with Ian.

Plus, I wouldn't have to be dealing with Mala's whole lust-in-the-woods/snake-bite/rash fiasco.

If, if, if.

Doctor Pennington popped his head into the waiting room and said, "Come on, Alex," about the time Uncle Brad and Aunt Charlotte came rushing in the entrance. I hung out off to the side while the doctor told my aunt and uncle that Mala was fine. She'd only need to take some antibiotics for a few days to clear up the rash.

Relieved of any duty I owed Mala by virtue of blood, and not in any mood to talk to her again, I turned to leave. Mala could deal with whatever her parents dished out on her own.

The guys must have overheard that Mala was okay, because the waiting room sat empty when I walked by. I trudged toward my Jeep, wanting nothing more than to bury my head under my pillow and forget this day had ever existed.

I went through the motions at work the next day. According to Grandma, Mala spent the day in bed recuperating from her ordeal. Sean had taken off some time to spend with his friends. The rest of the guys steered clear of me as much as possible, even Tommy. I wondered how much of it was the vibe I was giving off and how much was them wondering why I was so upset with Mala when I'd made out with a guy I barely knew in the woods, too. Whenever I noticed them talking among themselves, I imagined it was about me—and not in a good way. Let's just say I wasn't going to win any Miss Congeniality contests anytime soon.

I spent what time I wasn't helping customers thinking about my idea of getting away from Golden Bend and all the bad memories. What was left for me here anyway? Dad was gone, and my love for the river along with him. Mala and I were growing apart. And Sean and I were no closer to getting back together than we had been when he first arrived back here.

The day crawled by at a boring and excruciatingly slow pace, and I didn't expect much different when I woke again the next day. How many more days of summer were there?

But when I arrived at work the next day, Mala was already there, entering trip dates in the computer.

"This is new." I was pretty sure Mala had never beaten me to work.

"I had to get out of the house. Couldn't stand the Grand Stares of Disappointment anymore."

I didn't respond, just tossed my purse in the desk drawer, then walked to the front counter to check the day's schedule.

"Oh, and I'm feeling better, in case you were wondering," Mala said, sounding annoyed.

"Good," I said without turning to face her.

"Why did you bail on me at the hospital?"

"Your parents were there."

"Exactly."

I heaved a sigh and turned around. "You scared me half to death, Mala. I thought Austin had done something to you."

"I didn't have sex with him, you know."

"No, I didn't, but I don't really care."

"I can see that."

I crossed my arms and stared hard at her. "If I worried about you every time you did something stupid, I'd drive myself insane."

"I seem to remember you taking a trip into the woods too."

"Yes, but I didn't come out with a snakebite or an ass rash."

"It's on my *back*."

"Close enough."

Mala gave me an icy stare. "Listen, just because you haven't gotten with Sean doesn't give you the right to treat me like crap."

"This has nothing to do with Sean."

"Yeah, sure."

I opened my mouth to respond again but shut it when the mailman stepped in the front door to deliver a package too big for the mailbox. When he left, I didn't face Mala again.

Several seconds ticked by before I noticed Mala scratching her back out of the corner of my eye. "Why did you go off in the woods with Austin if you didn't want to?"

"Sometimes it feels good to be liked."

I glanced over my shoulder at Mala, who was staring at the computer. Her answer puzzled me. Everyone liked Mala. Then why had she sounded almost . . . sad?

"But don't worry," Mala said. "I've sworn off guys."

We'd see how long that lasted.

I reached for the phone when it rang. While I gave directions to some of today's rafters driving over from Grand Junction, Sean walked in. Beyond him, I noticed his friends standing outside. Oh yeah, he'd made plans to take them down the river today. Smart policy, them staying outside.

He glanced at me, and any look of support from the other night was gone. In its place was the same expression he'd had in his eyes when I'd come out of the woods with Ian. In the light of day, it was easier to identify now. It was like he didn't know me. He was a fine one to give disapproving looks. I mean, what exactly had he been doing with Ashlee all day yesterday? Talking about the state of world affairs?

As Sean left, he met Tommy coming in. A nod passed between them before Sean closed the door behind him. I finished the call as Tommy swiped a fruit tea from the fridge. "Remind me again—what's our company policy on dumping guests in the river?"

"It's frowned upon," Mala said without looking away from the computer.

I glanced outside, then back at Tommy. "No matter how much some guests might deserve it."

"Darn."

Any other day, I would have laughed as Tommy left to perform his nondunking job. But today didn't feel like a laughing day. Mala and I performed our duties with minimal conversation. If life didn't suck right now, I didn't know what did.

At lunch, I ran into town to pick up a pizza. When I returned, I found Daniel and Mala sitting across the desk from each other talking. I stopped just inside the door and stared. Had hell frozen over while I was gone?

Daniel looked up. "Oh good, lunch. I'm starving."

I watched the two of them over the next few minutes, but nothing much was said. I guessed Mala had found a way to make even Daniel feel sorry for her.

Since she kept working on the computer after we ate, I retreated outside. I checked gear, repainted our Cooley Mountain Whitewater sign out by the road, even refilled the air in the tires of the rental bikes.

"What's wrong?" Mala asked as she stepped out onto the porch.

"Just have a headache."

"Why don't you go home early? I can close up."

Part of me didn't want her to be nice to me, but I didn't argue. When I reached my grandparents' house, though, going inside held no appeal. Instead, I walked toward the woods that ran along the cliff above the river. They stretched all the way back to the barn where the party was supposed to be held. I had to admit, I wasn't exactly in a party mood. The horrible thought that Sean might invite his Denver friends to the party hit me. If he did, I wasn't going.

I walked slowly, listening to the river and trying to figure out what I should do about Sean. Tell him how I felt now, beg his forgiveness for last summer, and hope he didn't reject me and make the rest of my summer a nightmare? Wait to tell him at the party, when he'd already be in a good mood and I, hopefully, would be looking hot and irresistible? Or just forget the whole thing and move on?

My cell rang, startling me. When I looked at the display, I saw it was Mom calling me from Florida.

"Hey, Mom."

"Hello, sweetie. How are you?"

Truth or lie? "Okay." Lie. "You?"

"Good. I really am feeling better every day, stronger."

"I'm glad to hear that." And I was. I wished I could manufacture more excitement at the news, but I was feeling trampled and directionless.

"I miss you, Alex."

"I miss you too, Mom."

Then it hit me. Who did girls normally ask for dating advice when they didn't have big sisters? Their mothers. Mom said she was feeling better, but how would she react if I asked her about dating and love and guys? Would it make her think of Dad and send her back into depression? Or would it actually help, make her feel normal again? Maybe talking to Mom about the situation with Sean could help us both.

"Mom?"

When I got the "signal lost" tone, I cursed the spotty cell reception in the mountains. I walked around for five minutes trying to dial her back, but it was no use. The satellite had suddenly decided to point toward Jupiter or something.

I sank onto the cliff and pitched pebbles into the river below. Maybe this was God's way of telling me Mom wasn't ready for this discussion.

I looked up at the sky and wondered why nothing was connecting as it should. My phone and the satellite. Sean and me. I never thought I'd identify with a phone—searching for a connection that should be there but wasn't. How long would it continue to elude me? Or would it never click into place?

CHAPTER 12

When I ran out of pebbles within easy reach, I stood and meandered through the forest. Memories seemed to spring forth from the woods around me. Playing hide-and-seek at dusk. Picking wildflowers. Using ropes tied to tree limbs to swing out over the river, then letting go and anticipating the splash when we hit the water.

Staring at the tops of the aspens, I tripped over something. What the . . . ? Then I realized what I'd found—the remains of an old fort Sean and I had built when we were maybe ten years old. Just a couple of half-rotted logs remained, but the discovery still made me smile.

"You'll never take the fort!" I heard a much younger Sean proclaim in my memory. I closed my eyes and drifted back in time.

I had responded by hurling a huge snowball toward the fort like it was a cannonball. "The siege will not end until you surrender!"

The snowball splatted and exploded against the side of our fort.

"Ha! You missed."

Hey, I learn from my mistakes. The next time I let a snowball fly, I had another in reserve behind my back. Though the first one missed, when Sean popped back above the side of the fort he received the second one in the face.

I jumped up and down, squealing in triumph, until a hail of snowballs rained down on me from the fort. I lifted my arms to protect my head. When the attack stopped while he made more snowballs, I lifted my fist in the air and yelled, "Prepare to be overrun!"

I opened my eyes and stared at the rotting remains of Fort Landon. I'd insisted on the name since we'd built it on my grandparents' land.

I wandered around what remained of the fort, thinking through other fragmented memories. Sean and I had had a lot of fun playing out here back then. I wanted to go back to when things were simpler, before we became a couple, before his parents got divorced and he had to spend his school year in Denver with his mother and an entirely new set of friends like Ian and Ashlee. If I could have gone back, I'd have done things so differently.

Back in the fort days, we'd had no idea complications were ahead of us. All we'd cared about was playing wagon trail fort, skipping rocks, daring each other to jump into the river, and—hey, we'd buried a time capsule around here somewhere. I wondered where it was. I eyed the immediate area, trying to remember. The exact location didn't reveal itself, but I got a long, pointed limb and started digging. We'd been scrawny kids then. It couldn't have been buried very deeply.

Man, what had we put in that thing, anyway? I remembered we'd used Sean's old Spider-Man lunchbox to hold the contents. After half an hour of digging around, I finally gave up and decided to ask Sean if he recalled where we'd buried it. Who knew, maybe our shared past—the good parts anyway—would help swing things in my favor.

I couldn't turn off my brain. When I rolled over and looked at the clock, it read 11:59 p.m. No matter how many ways I considered to make things with Sean the way I wanted them, something made me kill the idea. They all came down to one thing—I was afraid. I kept imagining finally getting up the nerve to tell Sean that I was pretty sure I loved him and that I was the world's biggest idiot only to have him tell me that he didn't love me back, that I'd blown it.

I watched as twelve more endless minutes passed before I heard a thump outside my window. I crossed the room and peered out to find someone standing atop a ladder propped against the side of the house. I realized it was Tommy a moment before I screamed.

I opened the window. "What are you doing here?" I whispered.

"It's too nice a night to stay indoors."

I noticed movement on the ground. Tommy wasn't alone. I saw Mala first, then Daniel. Finally, Sean stepped out of the shadows. I had no idea how Sean or Mala felt about me being invited on whatever excursion Tommy had planned, but I was lost. I mean, what girl could possibly resist the sight of Sean Kenley in the moonlight? Plus, there was no

Ashlee attached to his side. In fact, there wasn't a Denverite in sight.

I looked back at Tommy. "Where are you going?"

"Down to the river."

My heart leapt to my throat. The need to make sure nothing bad happened at the river combined with the fact Sean would be part of the group convinced me to sneak out.

"Give me a minute to change."

Tommy didn't move.

I pointed toward the ground. "Down the ladder, Peeping Tommy."

He gave me a huge grin before starting down. At least he didn't look at me like I was seeking the crown of slutdom after my time with Ian.

After slipping into a T-shirt, shorts, and canvas mules, I opened the window wider and slipped out. When I reached the ground, Tommy and I stashed the ladder on the other side of the garage, where he'd found it. Feeling unexpectedly giddy, I hurried off into the night with my friends. We kept to the shadows so the nearly full moon didn't give us away. The wind wasn't stirring, but the familiar scent of pine still drifted on the air. The light of the moon bathed the landscape in a magical light, so much so that I wouldn't have been surprised to see fairies flitting through the glow.

My anxiety about Sean didn't go away, but it wasn't tying my insides into a pretzel anymore, either. Even though I could very well have gotten in trouble for sneaking out, this was the freest I'd felt in a while.

We kept the conversation to whispers and muffled

laughter until we got out of earshot of the house. We wandered along the edge of the pasture where Grandpa still kept a handful of cows. Their shapes stood out as darker blobs against the darkness of the night. I found myself wishing we'd stick to the woods and clearings, far from the river. Here I could enjoy myself without too much worry.

"So who would have thought the boss lady had a naughty girl inside?" Tommy teased as he walked backward in front of me.

"I've been known to thwart the rules now and again," I said, enjoying the group's mood.

"She just never gets caught," Mala said. "She has to keep her reputation as Miss Goody Two Shoes intact."

Though Mala sounded like she was teasing, a spiteful edge laced her voice. I knew she was referring to our time on the island.

"Don't know about you all, but I'm going swimming," Mala said all of a sudden, then started running toward the river off to our right. While I stood next to the cow pasture watching her disappear back into the trees, Tommy grabbed my hand and started off after her.

"No," I tried to say, but the fear built with each step toward the river, choking off my speech.

I managed a glance back to see Sean and Daniel following. I couldn't make out Sean's expression, but I wished he were the one holding my hand as we dashed through the night.

When we reached the river's edge, Mala was already in the river. Her clothes, minus her underwear, were strewn along the bank. Tommy quickly shucked his shirt and shorts and did a cannonball into the water.

"Your cousin's certifiable," Daniel said next to me as he pulled his shirt off. With a shake of his head, he dived in.

Though the moon lit the river, I stood in comparative darkness. All I could do was stare at the black, glassy expanse of the water. My heart beat so hard I felt the mad pulse against my eardrums. Now I knew how asthmatics felt when they couldn't get enough air into their lungs.

The river ran calm here, with no rapids, but it didn't matter. When I stared at it, all I saw was death.

Sean startled me when he placed his hand on my shoulder. "You don't have to do this," he said.

I shifted my gaze to him, and I didn't have to be able to see the color of his eyes to know exactly what they looked like. Something clicked inside me. I hated the idea of admitting my fear to him, of being less in his eyes. I wanted to be with him so much, and I wanted to conquer my fear of drowning. I'd lost too much, and now I was experiencing a desperate longing to get it back. I couldn't have my dad, but Sean and being able to run the river again were within the realm of possibility.

Before I could talk myself out of it, I pulled off my T-shirt and shorts and waded into the edge of the river. The water was cold, but I still broke out in a sweat and felt like I might pass out. I took a slow, deep breath and kept telling myself, *I can do this. I can do this.*

As I took another tentative step, feeling my way along the pebbly, muddy river bottom. I heard Sean tossing clothes behind me. One more step and he echoed my refrain. "You can do it," he said under his breath, where the others couldn't hear. By the time I stood in water high enough to cover my bra, I was shivering so much that my teeth cracked together. But instead of the cold, I focused all my concentration on where I placed my feet, making sure I had a solid footing. I couldn't manage to make my heart slow down.

"You're freezing," Tommy said as he swam toward me. "Let me warm you up."

Normally, his teasing helped lighten the mood, but right now I couldn't handle it. Moving quicker than I wanted to, I swam out of his path. "It's okay. I'll get used to the water temperature in a minute." If I didn't have a coronary first.

"You sure?" Tommy asked as he grinned and moved toward me again. This time, I slipped on a rock. But before I dropped below the surface of the water, someone strong grabbed me and set me back on sure footing again. I turned to find myself very close to Sean, close enough to kiss. I looked up into his eyes. Amidst its frantic beating, my heart performed a little jolt of joy, because Sean was looking back at me like he didn't hate me at all. Like he had looked at me last summer before Dad died. Like he might want to kiss me as much as I wanted to kiss him.

But the moment was lost when he suddenly got dunked in the river by Tommy, who laughed as he swam away.

Sean came up sputtering and flinging water. He pushed his wet hair back away from his face. Then he turned until he spotted Tommy. "Paybacks are hell, dude."

"So they say."

"This'll be fun," Sean said, giving Tommy a look like he was already planning the ultimate payback.

In the half-light, I couldn't tell whether Sean was teasing or really upset with Tommy. When Tommy floated farther away and started trying to dunk Mala, Sean turned to me again.

"You all right?"

I nodded, surprised at myself. It wasn't that the dark water around me didn't still terrify me, but I wasn't totally losing my mind, either. We stared at each other for a few seconds, both of us remembering those moments before he'd been dunked, and at least me trying to figure out how to recapture them. But they stayed lost for now. The possibility that they could exist again, however, thrilled me. One less obstacle to worry about. Next up—finding the right time to have the big talk about last summer.

For now, though, we all floated a little farther apart, able to enjoy the coolness of the river now that our bodies had acclimated to the temperature. I'm sure it was even relaxing for everyone else. Me, my muscles were too tense.

"So when are we having this barn party?" Tommy asked from several feet away.

I glanced at Sean and shrugged. "The Saturday after next might be good."

"I've got the music covered, so that officially gets me off the food list," Sean said.

"That right?" I asked. "I ought to assign you to make finger food just for saying that."

"We're supposed to have fun," Daniel said. "Not keel over from food poisoning."

"Funny," Sean said as he scooped water in his palm and slung it at Daniel. "Like you're any better."

"Didn't say I was."

Mala gave a dramatic huff. "I'll take care of the food," she said. "I wouldn't trust anything you guys made anyway."

"Guess that leaves me in charge of decorations," I said.

The conversation zipped back and forth: Who were we inviting? How were we going to pull it off without Grandma and Grandpa noticing? It kept my mind at least partially off the fact that I was standing in the river.

"Are your friends from Denver coming?" Mala asked in a detached sort of way that clearly told me she never wanted to see Austin again.

"No. They went home."

I glanced at Sean and found him watching me. Something about the moonlight, the cool water and warm air, seemed to make my senses so much more attuned to everything around me. That simple look felt like he was taking me in his arms and sharing his warmth and deepest feelings with me.

"I told them I was going to be really busy the next few days," he said, without breaking eye contact.

A smile tugged at the edges of my mouth, and I fought to keep it from spreading as wide as it wanted to. Ashlee was gone!

And if I wasn't badly mistaken, something was rekindling between Sean and me. That expression of disapproval was gone from his eyes, and I noticed him watching me several times. Plus, I was at least on the road to conquering my fear of the river. I eased through the water, lifting one foot slowly and placing it firmly on the river bottom before lifting the other. I didn't see myself stepping inside a raft anytime soon, but floating around in the shallows seemed to be doable.

"Hey, let's play Marco Polo," Mala said.

My stomach clenched not only at the idea of going into deeper water but also at the thought that I was about to make a fool of myself in front of Sean just when things were appearing to lean in my favor.

"I—"

Mala closed her eyes and called out, "Marco," before I could voice my objection.

"Polo," everyone responded. Everyone but me.

"Come on, Alex. No cheating," Mala said.

What was this—tough love? I couldn't imagine ever doing anything to make Mala so mad that she'd subject me to something like this. She knew how being in the water petrified me now. I was determined to power through, though, to remember how I used to love this same river. How fearless I'd been.

"Polo," I said low.

Mala surged toward me, but I somehow managed to scoot out of her way in time, causing her to career into Sean.

It took Sean longer to corral a victim, but he finally tagged Daniel.

"Damn," Daniel said as he shook the water from his shoulder-length hair.

"What are you, a dog?" Mala asked when droplets of the water hit her in the face.

Daniel raised a single eyebrow. "Little late to worry about getting wet."

Despite the anxiety stretching my nerves and tightening my muscles, I laughed a little at the exchange. There was no doubt who Daniel was going to try to tag. Mala knew it too, because as soon as he closed his eyes, she started wading farther away from him.

"Marco," he called.

"Polo" wasn't even out of our mouths before Daniel lunged toward Mala. She squealed and started splashing through the water to escape. She evaded him a couple of times, but then he leapt at her like a tiger and not only tagged her but also took her under the water for a full-body soaking.

The rest of us laughed as Mala kicked and tried to right herself.

"That's definitely the best one yet," Tommy said.

"Somehow I don't think Mala will agree with you," Sean added.

Daniel recovered first, then grabbed Mala's arms to pull her back above the water, held them close to his chest so she couldn't belt him.

She coughed and snorted water out of her nose. "You!"

"The game was your idea," Daniel said. "You dish it, you've gotta take it."

Mala struggled against Daniel's grip, and he just smiled in response. I focused on the two of them, wondering if the moonlight was making me imagine a moment of sexual tension between them. I glanced at Sean and Tommy, and the looks on their faces made me realize I hadn't imagined it. But when I looked back at Mala and Daniel, Mala had broken free and was swimming away from him. And Daniel's face was hidden by his hair.

I couldn't help a little laugh at the thought of those two together. Could there be a more ill-matched pair? They'd drive each other insane in fifteen minutes flat. It'd serve them and their bickering right if they ended up liking each other.

I shook my head. Sparks or not, I'd believe them as a couple when I saw it.

Despite a few funny and interesting moments, my fear skyrocketed when Tommy tagged me as I retreated to shallower water. Then it was my turn, and the distance between me and anyone I could tag seemed like miles. I closed my eyes as the game required, but my throat constricted and my hands went numb. I imagined my dad's last moments in life, fighting this very river before it took him under, then threw him out like so much trash.

I concentrated on breathing slowly as I edged farther out, making sure at least one of my feet stayed in contact with the river bottom at all times. I would conquer this fear—I would!

I wasn't very good at the game, but I managed not to fall. I became hyperaware of where I placed my feet on an area of smooth, round stones on the river's bottom.

"Any day now," Mala taunted me.

"So anxious to be It again, Mala?" Tommy asked.

I made a grab for Tommy, but he eluded me easily. Same with Daniel. Sean had the decency to utter a little "Sorry" before he stepped to the side.

"Ugh!" I grew more determined to tag one of them as I gained a little more confidence. "One of you is going down."

"Oh, come on, you can do better than that," Tommy said as I swung out my arm toward the sound of his laughter and missed.

"You're not even trying," Mala said.

Maybe in her warped way she was trying to help me, but something about the way she said it made my teeth clench. I *was* trying. Hell, I was in the river, wasn't I? I wouldn't have thought this possible only a few hours ago.

Since Mala was the one who'd gotten me into this, it seemed only appropriate that she be the one I took down. I focused on the sound of her voice, repositioned my feet, and lunged.

One of my feet slipped off the rock underneath it, and I hit the water face-first. Panic consumed me as I sank below the surface. I thrashed and tried to right myself. Oh God! I opened my mouth to shout and swallowed water instead.

I clawed at the inky water around me, but I couldn't see which way was up. Everything looked black and sinister.

Then someone's hands grabbed me and pulled me to the surface. Panic still raced through me like a potent drug, and I rushed for the shore, to the safety of dry land. I didn't even pause to see who'd saved me. My pulse banged so loudly I couldn't hear what everyone was yelling at me. All I could think was, *Get out of the water.*

When I crawled up on shore, I somehow remembered to grab my clothes before running into the woods. I didn't look back. I thought I might keep running until I'd left Golden Bend and the river behind forever.

I stumbled through the bushes into the thin stand of trees lining the river. More tears popped into my eyes when my naked foot landed on something prickly. I stopped only long enough to pull on my clothes and shoes, then started hurrying toward the dirt lane that led from the house to the barn. I increased my pace when I heard running behind me. Mortified, I couldn't face any of them now.

"Alex! Wait up!" called Sean.

Of all of them, he was the one I really and truly couldn't face now. I had to accept that I wasn't the person he once liked. That carefree river runner was gone, and there was no future for us. I couldn't accept those truths if I had to look into his eyes.

Desperation fueled my retreat, but Sean still caught me. His fingers wrapped around my arm, pulling me to a stop. I cried out, "No," in a pained voice, a voice that hardly sounded like my own.

Sean turned me slowly to face him, but I didn't make eye contact. I wanted to disappear into the cloak of the surrounding night.

"It's okay," he said in a soothing tone.

I shook my head. "It's not okay. It's never going to be okay again." Why couldn't he see he was making it worse by not letting me go?

"It will."

"How?" I screamed. Even in my current state, I wasn't immune to the tenderness in his expression—or to how wonderful he looked without a shirt on, his skin and dark hair wet. I lowered my voice. "How will anything ever be normal again?"

"You'll get back to the river—you'll see."

I shook my head. "I can barely breathe when I think about it. It's like someone's squeezing my throat, or I've swallowed a baseball." I stepped away and gestured angrily toward the river beyond the trees. "When I look at it now, I want it to dry up."

"Alex, listen to yourself," he pleaded. "You've rafted this river hundreds of times. So have tens of thousands of other people. Sometimes accidents happen. It's like we tell the tourists—it's more likely you'll be in a car accident than a rafting one."

I glanced back at Sean and felt intensely, profoundly tired. "But my heart doesn't nearly beat out of my chest when I look at the highway."

Sean sighed. "Your father wouldn't want this for you."

All my wretched feelings about Sean, my dad, Mala, everything bottled up inside me picked that moment to explode. "*You* have no idea what my dad would want! Don't pretend you do." My voice cracked and I looked up at the sky to keep my tears at bay. "Nobody knows, because he's dead."

"Alex, don't."

"Don't what?" I asked, my words sharp and venomous.

"It's just going to take time to get back to where you were."

Time? It'd been nearly a year, and I was probably more frightened tonight than I'd ever been. What I needed was a new life far away from everything that reminded me of all I'd lost.

I shook my head. "You don't understand. No one does."

This time, Sean didn't stop me as I walked away.

CHAPTER 13

I dragged myself to work the next morning figuring I might as well get the brunt of my embarrassment over with instead of dreading it. Despite the fact that I felt like I hadn't slept in a week, and probably looked like it too, I decided to ride my bike to work instead of driving. I hoped the fresh morning air and exercise would help lift my mood. I listened to the latest Pottercast podcast on my iPod, hoping my mind wouldn't wander. So didn't work.

After I'd left Sean standing alone in the middle of the night, I'd realized that instead of seizing the opportunity to tell him how I felt about him and apologizing for last summer, I'd lashed out at him.

This morning, I felt like someone had wrung me out and hung me up to dry.

Maybe things would be simpler if I just resolved to forget Sean, to forget about dating altogether. I might be too much of a mess to figure out how to do it properly. Most of this summer so far I'd felt like a seesaw about Sean—upbeat and hopeful one minute, full of doubt and frustration the next. My brain must be cracked.

When Mala came in, I tried to appear busy answering e-mail. But she came over and sat on the edge of the couch facing me anyway.

"Alex?"

"Um?" I said without looking away from the computer screen.

"I'm sorry about last night." She sounded genuine in her apology, but I still felt raw.

I shifted my gaze to her. "Which part? When you suggested we go swimming when you know how I feel about the river? Or maybe when you taunted me when I didn't play up to your standards?"

She got to her feet and took several steps before stopping, facing me, and crossing her arms. "All of it, okay? Can you please just accept my apology?"

Part of me wanted to make her grovel more, but a much larger part was so tired of being at odds with everyone. "Fine. Apology accepted."

"So," Mala started tentatively, "what happened with Sean after you left?"

I shrugged. "Not much. He asked if I was okay. I said I'd be fine, and I left." I didn't feel like sharing more than that, too weary to do more than gloss over what had been said. What good would it do to rehash it anyway?

To redirect her attention, I said, "So, what was that moment with Daniel last night?"

"Daniel?"

"Yes, you remember. Tall guy, blond hair," I said, forcing a lightness I didn't feel into my words.

Mala gave me a "don't be a smart-ass" look. "What are you talking about?"

"I believe it's commonly called attraction."

"When did you start smoking crack?"

"Hey, I'm just telling you what I saw."

Mala placed her hands on her hips and stared at me. "It was dark, and you were freaked."

"I'm not the only one who noticed."

Mala threw her arms up in exasperation. "Then you're all smoking crack."

Strange how this conversation was actually improving my mood. I leaned back in my chair. "Doth she protest too much?"

"Oh, seriously, he and I have nothing in common."

"You work together."

"Exactly! We're coworkers. He's quiet, I'm not. He reads things like Thoreau for fun. I'm more of a *Cosmo* girl."

"Why are you so afraid of everyone identifying you as something more than that?"

Mala scrunched up her forehead. "Huh?"

"You get good grades. I know you're not dumb. Why don't you let people see that side of you?"

Mala turned and started doodling on a notepad atop the front counter. "I don't feel like advertising it. I'd rather go out and have fun."

I sighed. "Being smart does not equate to not having fun."

"You seen a queue of dates lining up for Callie Whidmore?" she asked, naming the Girl Most Likely to be Valedictorian.

"I'm not talking about Callie."

"No. You're attempting to divert the conversation away from you and Sean."

I looked away from her. "There is no 'Sean and me.'"

"Because you're not trying hard enough. Kick Ashlee's skinny ass. Drag Sean into the back room and have your wicked way with him."

"I'm not sure trying to get Sean back is the right thing to do anymore." I leaned my head back against the chair and stared at the ceiling beams for a moment. "I don't think I can stay here much longer. I've been thinking about this for a long time, and I think everyone will be better off if we sell the business and move away from the bad memories."

Mala didn't say anything. Her face was slack with shock. "Sell the rafting business? It's been in our family for decades."

Her reaction surprised me, seeing as how I'd never pegged her as liking Cooley Mountain Whitewater for anything beyond her paycheck and a way to meet hot guys. That and the fact that Aunt Charlotte hadn't gone into the family business. She owned a coffee shop in town instead. "I think it's best."

"Best for who?"

"Everyone."

"Everyone, or just you? When were you planning on springing this gem?" She sounded mad now, hurt. So much for our reconciliation.

"I don't know. End of this summer, maybe. You've got to see how it will help. I obviously can't run the business—not beyond the office, anyway. Every time I look at the river, I imagine. . . . Plus, Grandma and Grandpa are getting older. And Mom, well, I don't think it's good for her to be here."

"And what about me?"

"You?"

"Don't sound so shocked. It never even crossed your mind to ask me how I feel about this place, did it?"

"I never got the impression it was your great passion to run Cooley Mountain."

"It would have been nice to be asked before you started making decisions for the whole family." Mala slammed the pen against the counter and paced across the office section of the cabin. "What about the good memories?"

"They're hard to remember."

Mala stared at me like she didn't know me. "I never thought I'd see the day when you'd give up. All these months, I thought you just needed time to get over Uncle Steve's death." She shook her head in disgust. "Why'd you even worry about Sean when you were going to sabotage any hint of interest he showed?"

"I haven't!"

"Haven't you? I mean, why try when you're just going to leave all of us behind anyway?" Anger reddening her pretty face, Mala slammed out the back door, leaving me wondering if there was any truth to her accusation.

Was I self-destructing? And was I taking down everyone around me at the same time?

CHAPTER 14

Mala left work early, still mad at me. Not that I was surprised. Everything else I touched seemed to turn to crap—why not the relationship with my cousin and best friend?

After I locked up for the day, I headed home on my bike, wishing I could truly *go home* instead of to my grandparents' house. I wanted to sleep in my own bed, pull clothes out of my own closet, sit on my own back porch. And I desperately wanted my life to be normal again, to ride into the driveway and see my dad sitting on the cedar swing he'd built in our front yard.

A fresh wave of sadness hit me, the accompanying dizziness and punch to my heart making me swerve dangerously close to the road. If I left Golden Bend and everything that was familiar, would I really be able to escape the bad memories? A different kind of memory surfaced—one of Dad's little truths.

"Running away from your problems won't solve them," he'd told me the one time I'd given in to temptation and cheated on a test. I'd gotten caught and never wanted to go back to school. I could hear Dad's voice, every inflection, in my head.

But he couldn't have foreseen what I'd been through the past year when he uttered those words, could he?

I heard a car approaching behind me and steered my bike as far off to the side of the road as I could.

The car slowed, and I thought the driver might be pulling into one of the two side roads I'd just passed. But then he sped up again before slowing beside me. I realized I recognized the sound of the car's engine. I looked over as Sean rolled down his passenger-side window.

The wind blew his hair, a bit longer now than at the beginning of the summer. I liked the new length, the sun-kissed highlights. When he reached up to push it behind his ear, I imagined him doing the same to mine.

"Can we talk?" he asked.

Embarrassment swamped me, and I almost veered into the trees on the side of the road. "I'm tired. I just want to go home."

"It'll only take a minute."

"Not today."

"Come on, Alex," he said as someone in a mammoth SUV pulled up behind him and started honking.

"Okay, okay," I said, more to make sure he wasn't a victim of road rage than out of any sudden desire to talk. I hadn't yet figured out how I'd manage an apology strong enough to cover how badly I'd treated him not once, but twice now.

He steered the car off the road at one of the many

pullouts designed as river access points for kayakers and hikers. I stopped but didn't get off the bike. Sean walked over to me, then nodded at a concrete picnic table at the edge of a stand of pines.

I propped the bike against a tree and followed him to the table. We sat side by side, our backs against the table. The silence weighed down on me, like the air surrounding us was made of lead. Even among the pine and forest smells scenting the air, I smelled him—his clean, warm, distinctive Sean scent that made me want to nuzzle his neck.

"I'm sorry I wasn't more understanding last night," he said. "I know 'It's going to be okay' probably isn't what you needed to hear. It's just one of those things people say when they don't know what else to say."

"I know." I tried to keep myself uncaring and distant, to protect what little seemed to be left of my heart, but the ache in my chest felt like it was going to consume me. "After Dad died, I started having nightmares. About him drowning. Like I was there, drowning too." I shook my head, knowing this all sounded overdramatic. "I couldn't breathe. It was so scary." I met Sean's eyes. "I felt like that last night. I know it's totally irrational, but I can't seem to get over it."

"It's not irrational." He stared at the ground in front of him. "I mean, I get it."

I stared at his profile, the strong jaw, his thick eyelashes, how a lighter section of his hair curved below his ear, until he looked back at me. "Why are you so nice to me? After everything I said to you?"

He shrugged, and I could tell from the expression on his face that he knew I was talking about last summer and not last night. "You were hurting."

"But . . ." My voice cracked. I had to swallow. "But when I blamed you, I couldn't have been more wrong. It was my choice to be with you that day instead of going to work." I turned my attention to the bark of the nearest pine tree and finally admitted what I'd kept festering inside of me for months. "I was so tired of trying to reach him, to find some part of him that was the same as he used to be. When he died, I felt so guilty. Like if I'd tried harder, I could have . . . I don't know. . . . Maybe he wouldn't have been so depressed. If I'd gone with him that day, I could have saved him."

Sean reached over and took my hand in his larger, warmer one. "It wasn't your fault."

I looked back at him with fat tears blurring my vision. I wanted to believe him. "Sean, I'm so sorry for saying those awful things. Sometimes I can't believe I told you that it was your fault Dad died, that I wished I'd never met you. I knew as soon as I said it that it wasn't true. I just didn't know how to take it all back."

Sean rubbed his thumb back and forth over the back of my hand. "You just did."

"I really am sorry."

"I know."

"You're being too easy on me. I deserve for you to hate me forever."

"What should I do, make you beg and grovel?"

"Yes."

Sean laughed at that. "I've got a better idea. Won't be easy, though."

I examined his face, trying to figure out what he might be about to say. Nervousness welled in me, making me jittery. But it was a nervousness tinged with hope. "What?"

"We could go swimming after work, just the two of us, so there's not pressure from anyone else."

I stiffened and pulled my hand out of his. "No."

"Why not?" He asked it gently, like he truly wanted to understand.

"You saw me last night. I think my days of enjoying the river are over."

Sean shifted so that he was facing me. His look of understanding and determination seemed impossible, but that's what I saw.

"I don't believe that," he said. "You just have to want it enough. Don't you want to get back on the river?"

The question reverberated in my head. Images of me rafting mixed with ones of me leaving Golden Bend behind.

I stared into his eyes, my heart aching that I wasn't able to leap at this opportunity to spend time with him. "I don't know."

"Tell you what, I'll be at the beach area a half hour after work tomorrow. You can come if you want, or not. No pressure."

For several seconds I was unable to speak. "Even if I tried, I'm not sure it'd work."

"Won't know until you try."

I gave him a sad smile. That was another of my dad's

favorite truths. I remembered how I'd teased him by calling him Cliché Man, and how he'd said some sayings were clichés because they were true.

"Why are you doing this after how horrible I've been?" I asked.

"We've been friends a long time, Alex. Friends help each other."

My heart sank. Friends. He wouldn't say it, but he was offering to help me overcome my fear because he pitied me, not because he wanted to get back together.

Out of pride, I felt like telling him I didn't need his help. But I also didn't want to refuse his olive branch, this opportunity to move beyond what had passed between us at the end of last summer.

"Okay."

"Okay?"

"I'll give it a try." I'd spend time with Sean, even though I knew my heart would be breaking every moment we were alone together and I was reminded of how much I loved him. And how he didn't love me back.

With each tick of the clock toward closing time, I wondered why I'd agreed to face my fear of the water head-on with Sean. I must have lost my mind temporarily yesterday afternoon. Sure, I wished I wasn't afraid of the water. I mean, who liked having a phobia? But to have the guy you really like offer to help you get over it? That was just embarrassing. Not to mention the whole chipping-away-at-my-heart aspect.

To keep from watching the second hand creep around

the clock, I headed outside to stow the bikes for the night. Of course, that allowed me to see Sean, who was helping Tommy and Daniel put away the last of today's rafting gear. When our eyes met for a moment, my nervousness mushroomed and I considered calling off our secret rendezvous. It was nice that he'd suggested we keep it secret to save me more embarrassment than I'd already suffered. After all, there was a high likelihood I'd fail miserably and make an even bigger fool of myself.

Mala, however, refused to meet my eyes as she returned from gassing up the Cooley Mountain Whitewater van and parked it in its customary spot. She slipped out of the van, shoved her iPod earphones in her ears, and started humming the latest Leona Lewis song. She was still mad at me, and every attempt I'd made to talk to her had been rebuffed. It was like I was already gone to her. Part of me was saddened by our argument, while another part wanted to yell at her to stop pouting and try to understand. Sure, we'd fought before. But up until this summer, we'd never had so many spats.

I was still trying to figure out what Mala's big hairy deal was when I came out of the bike storage shed to find Tommy waiting for me.

"Are you okay?" he asked.

"Yeah. Why?"

He shrugged. "I don't know. You've seemed about half here the past couple of days."

I walked past him. "Just a lot on my mind."

"This about the other night?" he asked as he fell into step beside me.

I glanced over at him and wondered why I couldn't like Tommy as more than a friend. He was good-looking in that blonde, athletic, sure-of-oneself way. He was definitely funny, had a great accent, flirted with the best of them. I doubted he'd say no if I showed interest. Things would certainly be simpler with someone like Tommy.

"I really don't want to talk about it."

"Okay." He kept walking beside me. "I've got a yearning for Mama Rosa's pizza tonight. Want to come?"

I stopped at the edge of the cabin's porch. "Sorry, can't. I've got to run some errands for my grandmother and call my mom."

Fate must have a wicked sense of humor, because Mala picked that moment to walk by on the way to her car. For the first time all day, her eyes met mine. Judging by her narrowed eyes, she knew I was lying. I held my breath, thinking she would reveal that fact to Tommy, but she looked away and kept walking.

Tommy noticed the silent exchange. Actually, I'm pretty sure the people on the International Space Station could have seen it. He leaned close and said, "You can't resist me forever." He winked at me.

He certainly could make me laugh, which no one else had managed to do lately. "Is that a fact?"

"Known worldwide."

I laughed again and pushed him toward his aunt's car. "I think they ran you out of England because your ego got too big."

He turned and walked backward, smiled like the devil, and blew me a kiss. "I shall add you to my legions of fans."

I rolled my eyes as I stepped onto the porch to lock the front door.

When I'd mentioned doing errands for my grandmother, that actually hadn't been a total lie. I did have to drop off the electric payment at the co-op and pick up some yarn from the little knitting shop. Granted, that all took me about ten minutes total, but I wasn't telling anyone about my meeting with Sean. I didn't want to answer the questions I knew would result or have an audience to my humiliation if the swimming didn't work out.

When I left Flying Needles and headed for the beach area where we'd had the bonfire and the ill-fated game of spin the bottle, my stomach started rolling. By the time I pulled into the parking area and cut the engine, I had begun to seriously doubt my sanity and was considering making a run for it.

Sean's car already sat in the front space. I stared at it for a full minute. I closed my eyes and remembered a certain moonlit night last summer, one not unlike a couple of nights ago at the river. Only Sean had driven us higher into the mountains and pulled over at a scenic overlook.

"Come on," he had said as he opened my door and took my hand. "I want to show you something."

My heart beat wildly, a hummingbird fighting to free itself from captivity. I loved the strong, warm feel of Sean's hand wrapped around mine as we followed a narrow dirt path away from the parking area through some thick pines.

After a couple of minutes, we came to a gap in the trees. In the valley far below, the lights of Golden Bend winked back at us. I could even see the reflection of the moon in the bend of the river that gave our hometown its name.

"It's beautiful up here," I said.

"I thought you'd like it." Sean led me a few steps forward to a natural ledge. When we seated ourselves, he wrapped his arm around my shoulders and drew me close. I lay my head on his shoulder.

"This is nice," I said after a few moments of soaking in the wonder of being this close to Sean, the romance of the spot and the night surrounding us.

"Just nice?" he whispered against my temple.

I lifted my head and looked up at him. "Maybe a little bit better than nice."

"Looks like I have to do some convincing to up your rating." He smiled before lowering his lips to mine and kissing me.

Now, a year later, I could still feel the warmth of that kiss. How it made my body tingle all over and never want to leave that spot above the world. I pushed away the thought that I'd never feel that way again.

I took a slow, deep breath and looked through the trees toward the river. I could do this.

Okay, I was less sure I could manage this with each step I took away from my Jeep toward the river. I felt like throwing up. When the river came into view, I stopped and listened to the familiar sound of its flow. I forced myself to remember the days before Dad had reported for National Guard duty, back when the river was as much a part of our lives as eating and sleeping. I deliberately called up the thrill, the love, the way I'd never even considered moving away from this place and lifestyle. It all seemed so long ago, longer than the actual passage of months. Even if I managed to get back to being able to swim without total terror, I didn't know if I could recapture my love for the river. I wasn't sure I wanted to. It might be time to move on to some other kind of life.

But I'd think about that later. I managed to make my feet move forward again.

"I wondered if you'd actually come," Sean said from his perch on a log when I walked into view.

"So did I." I stared at the water, too nervous and embarrassed to make eye contact.

"You can do this, you know."

"We'll see."

When Sean stood and stripped off his shirt, I swallowed hard. The sight of him without a shirt always did crazy things to my heart rate, and sent very naughty thoughts zinging through my head. My mother would have been shocked. Mala would have hooted her approval—well, if she hadn't been mad at me.

And if Dad had still been here, he'd have locked me in my room until I turned forty.

I'd come this far. I might as well try. Sean had already seen me at my worst anyway, right? I pulled my shirt and shorts off, leaving my simple, blue, one-piece bathing suit. When I turned back toward the river, Sean was already submerged up to his waist. With another deep breath, I edged my way into the water. No matter how many times I'd been in this river, the first few moments of cold were always a shock.

"Doing good," Sean said, encouraging me into deeper water.

Concentrating on forcing myself to breathe slowly, I took one careful step after another, so aware of my foot placement that my surroundings other than Sean and the river disappeared. I didn't want a repeat of my slip and consequent freak-out. A girl could only stand so much embarrassment in her life. Plus if I had another close call, I was so moving to the middle of the desert, where they barely had enough water to drown a worm.

We kept moving at the caterpillar pace for what seemed like forever before Sean spoke again. "Now lift your feet and float."

I froze, irrational fear flooding me and making my body go cold and numb. "I can't."

"Yes, you can," Sean said in a way that was gentle and encouraging, not accusatory or pitying. "You've been swimming since you were tiny."

True, but back when I had short, chubby legs, I hadn't had a clue what the river was capable of, what it could take away. I wished desperately to be back on the riverbank.

Sean swam closer to me, then held out his hand. "Do you trust me?"

I looked into his eyes and knew that I not only trusted him, but I loved him too, so much it hurt. Could I really

leave Golden Bend behind without telling him that? I mentally shook my head. Now wasn't the time to think those
thoughts. I had to concentrate on not going under. I looked
down at the water flowing past my body. Why couldn't anything, just one thing, be easy?

I tried to hide how much panic had me in its grip as I
lifted my hand and placed it in Sean's. As he grasped it, I
wondered if he could feel mine shaking.

"Believe you can do it," he said, then started backing up,
forcing me to follow.

When we reached water up to my neck, my airway constricted, making it impossible to draw enough breath. My
eyes widened as I imagined being swept away, bashed against
boulders by the rapids downstream.

I started flailing, crazed to free myself from the river.

Without saying anything, Sean guided me back to waist-
deep water and held onto my arms until my feet settled
firmly on the ground and the terror subsided.

"I'm sorry," I whispered.

"Don't be," he said in such a kind, understanding tone it
nearly made me weep.

I lowered my arms from his and stared down at the surface of the water, unable to look him in the face. "I can't do
this."

"You can. Don't be so hard on yourself. You don't have to
be perfect on the first day."

I exhaled. "Easy for you to say."

"It's not easy at all."

I made myself meet his eyes.

"I hate seeing you so afraid of the river," he said. "I know how much you used to love it."

I swallowed against the uncomfortable lump in my throat. He might not love me anymore, but it touched me deeply that he still cared as a friend. That he still knew me so well.

We stood in the shallow water a few more moments before Sean asked, "Ready to try again?"

The numbness pricked at my fingertips trailing in the water. I closed my eyes and mentally cursed the entire situation.

"Here," Sean said.

When I opened my eyes, he was holding out both of his hands to me.

"Hang on. I promise I won't let go of you."

My heart hitched at his words, wishing they meant more than they did. I took a deep breath, resolving to try one more time. I placed my hands in Sean's.

I inched forward, following him, doing my best to breathe in and out at something approximating a normal pace. My foot slipped on a slick rock and I slid down until I was neck-deep.

"Oh God!"

"You're okay," Sean said as he held onto me while I found my footing again.

I fought tears. "I really don't think I can do this."

"Don't think," Sean said. "Go with your instinct."

"My instinct is telling me to move to Nevada."

He laughed a little, easing the tension a fraction. "You wouldn't be happy in Nevada."

I glanced at his face before looking away again. Confusion bubbled up inside me. When I was with Sean like this, I didn't want to move away, even with the phobia and bad memories threatening to choke me. The stubborn hope of being with him again was the one thing preventing me from broadcasting my intent to move far away to the rest of my family.

For the next few minutes, we stayed in the calmer edge of the river. I kept hoping I'd relax, but my nerves were fraying and my muscles were so tense that I felt more like a floating log than a human. When Sean started guiding me toward the area of the river with the swifter current, I balked and started treading water.

"You can't stay in the safe parts," he said.

"Yes, I can."

"Not to really get beyond this."

I'd have hated his gentle insistence if I hadn't known he was right. If I hadn't realized he cared enough to insist.

"Maybe I don't want to."

He stared at me, like he was dissecting my thoughts. "That's not you talking," he said. "That's the fear."

"Yeah, well, it's part of me now."

"Only because you let it be."

"You think I want to be so pathetic?"

"Maybe."

"Yeah, because embarrassing myself is so near the top of my list of life goals."

He stayed quiet for several seconds, his expression making it appear as though he were debating saying something. "You've got to do this or you'll never get over your dad's death."

The familiar sharp pain that always accompanied the words *dad's death* clawed at my middle. I couldn't do this anymore. I slipped my hands out of Sean's and started for the bank as fast as I could move, but Sean latched onto me. When he pulled me back toward him, I ended up very, very close to him, looking up into his hypnotic eyes.

He was going to kiss me. I knew it. Despite the chilly water, my entire body warmed in anticipation. It'd been so long since we'd kissed. I longed to taste him again, to feel him pressed close to me.

When he swam away a couple of strokes, I thought my heart might shatter all over again. How many times could a heart break before it was irreparable?

"Maybe that's enough for today," he said and pointed toward the bank.

Odd that I didn't want to swim toward it anymore. I wanted him to look at me again with that hungry, yearning expression I'd seen in his eyes for a few wonderful seconds. I wanted him to grab me and plant the kiss to end all kisses on my lips, to make me forget where I was and why I was afraid to be here.

Instead, we reached the riverbank and he helped me out of the water, my wet legs shaking. Again, he looked at me as if he were thinking about more than he was saying.

"Sean—"

"Same place and time tomorrow?" he asked, cutting me off.

"Sure." I even forgot that he was talking about tackling the river again as I answered.

We wrung water from our hair and slipped our clothes back on in silence. I couldn't help but feel that he was on the verge of saying something important. But he didn't. As we walked back toward the parking area, I once again wondered if it might be best for us to stay friends. Simpler. Less confusing.

As I slipped into my Jeep, I noticed Sean eyeing me from his car. Was he waging the same mental battle? There must be a part of him that was still attracted to me. There had to be! If I felt such a powerful pull toward him simply by watching him across a parking lot, he had to feel it too. He just had to.

CHAPTER 15

I was so wrapped up in my thoughts when I arrived home, it was a good thing I didn't also have to think of a way to explain my wet hair to my grandparents. They'd gone to Denver to take Mala's parents to the airport. That whole situation was probably adding to Mala's sour mood. Her parents were off to Napa and San Francisco for vacation without her. Granted, it was their anniversary trip, but she was still miffed she wasn't getting to go.

Maybe after I showered and changed, I'd give her a call, suggest a pizza-and-movie night as a peace offering.

As I stepped in the back door, I saw that a phone call wouldn't be necessary. Mala sat at the kitchen table drinking a fruit tea and reading an actual book. That was new. I started to comment on it, but I noticed the darkness of her mood when she closed the copy of *Emma* and gave me a probing look.

"Where have you been?" she asked.

"Nowhere," I answered, bristling at her accusatory tone.

"Did it rain in Nowhere?"

I walked the rest of the way into the kitchen and dropped

the bag of yarn on the table. "I decided to go swimming, okay? I'm trying to get over my fear of the water."

"By yourself? After how you reacted last night?"

"Yes, by myself. Didn't really want witnesses."

Mala still looked suspicious, but I didn't want to share the truth. I wanted to keep whatever was between Sean and me between us, something that I could hold close and not share with every member of my family. Plus, the relationship felt fragile right now, like it might disintegrate if I mentioned it to someone. Mala might not have been totally convinced, but at least she didn't question me further.

"Where's your car?" I asked with care, as though Mala were a bomb and I might accidentally set her off with a wrong word.

"At home. Seems Mom has been reading parenting books and suddenly realized she needs to punish me for that night on the island. Getting bitten by a snake and being humiliated evidently aren't enough. I have to stay here without my car for the next two weeks while they're gone."

A twinge of guilt made me wince inwardly. After all, I'd made out with a guy I didn't really know, too, and had not been punished. Of course, my grandparents didn't know about that, and I planned on keeping it that way.

Mala's banishment to the ranch wasn't only an annoyance for her. No car meant I'd been wordlessly appointed her chauffeur, whether I liked it or not. That was going to make continuing to meet Sean for defeat-the-phobia lessons difficult. Great.

The ensuing silence grew awkward, so I took the bag

of yarn and walked into the living room. I placed the new skeins in the basket next to Grandma's chair. When I turned around, Mala stood in the doorway to the kitchen watching me.

"What?"

She continued to stare for a moment, then shook her head and retraced her steps.

I stood in the living room listening to her bang around in the kitchen. What I really wanted to do was go to my room and let her continue to stew, but I was really tired of her animosity. I let out a sigh, then headed toward the kitchen.

The book was nowhere in sight, but a countertop full of baking ingredients was.

"What are you making?"

"A cake."

"You know Grandma's going to kill you for putting sweets in front of Grandpa."

"You only live once, so I think you should get what you want and enjoy it to the fullest." Mala's Philosophy on Life 101. "Take you and Sean, for instance."

"I swear you could turn a conversation on world economic policy to guys."

She shrugged. "Hey, maybe there are some cute economists out there somewhere. You can find one when you move away." I could tell she was trying to hold onto her anger, but her natural bubbly personality was fighting it.

I chose to ignore the cutting remark. "*Cute* isn't the first word that comes to mind."

"Okay, never mind economists." Mala broke two eggs

into the other cake ingredients. "Do you still want to get back with Sean?"

I grabbed the eggshells and tossed them into the trash. "I don't know what I want anymore. And I can't tell if he might want to be more than friends."

"I know one guy who wants to be more than friends."

"Huh?"

Mala glanced at me while stirring the batter. "Tommy. It's obvious he has a huge crush on you."

"Because he flirts with me? He flirts with anything with boobs."

Mala heaved a sound of exasperation and turned her attention to pouring the batter into two cake pans. "Believe whatever you want."

Ugh, why couldn't we have a conversation anymore without her getting irritated?

"I could say the same thing to you."

"Is this the Daniel thing again?"

I gestured toward where she'd been sitting when I came home. "Noticed you were reading earlier. That have anything to do with him?"

Mala snorted. "It's not the first time I've read a book, you know."

"But it's summer, and that one's suspiciously thick."

"Quit trying to divert the conversation," she said as she bent to slide the pans into the oven.

"Why are you so resistant to the idea of Daniel liking you?"

She stood to her full height and propped one hand against

her hip. "Because that's about as likely as *Cosmo* giving up quizzes."

"It might be more likely if you stopped sitting in Tommy's lap and riding off on D. J. Forrester's motorcycle. If you gave it a chance."

Mala's jaw tightened. "Seriously, Alex, I don't think you're the best person to be giving dating advice. You're too chicken to go after the guy you want, and you don't even notice when another one has it so bad for you he follows you around like a puppy dog."

Mala strode into the living room and clicked on a rerun of *Gossip Girl*. I sank into one of the chairs at the table and stared at the opposite wall. Had I been misinterpreting Tommy's flirting all these weeks? Was there more there than just Tommy being Tommy? Things he'd said and done, the latest being his asking me out to pizza at Mama Rosa's, clicked into place.

I propped my elbows against the table and dropped my head into my upturned hands.

I pressed hard against my temples and suppressed the urge to scream. Gah, everything was so messed up, playing out so wrong. So very wrong.

CHAPTER 16

As I drove Mala and myself to work the next morning, I thought about what she'd said regarding Tommy liking me and wondered how I should handle the situation. I could try to ignore him as much as possible, but that seemed unworkable, especially since I still considered him a friend. I could cool my interactions with him, be very aware of not saying anything that could be misconstrued. But I didn't want to make it obvious I knew, either. Maybe it was best to just find a balance between being distant and being too flirtatious, to take it one day at a time through the rest of the summer.

I'd act like a friend, nothing more. Oh, the irony.

Once we arrived at the office, I had a whole five minutes before Tommy came in, perched atop my desk as he liked to do, and gave me a sad basset hound look. "It was terribly lonely without you at dinner last night."

I lifted my eyebrows. "You went to Mama Rosa's by yourself?"

"Yes, I was quite pitiful sitting there all alone."

"You," I said, pointing at him, "are full of crap."

He placed his hand against his heart. "You wound me."

I hated being uncomfortable around Tommy, but his words seemed loaded with new meaning now. They weren't just harmless teasing anymore.

I noticed Sean heading in the door as Tommy spoke. Had Sean noticed Tommy's feelings for me as well? Could that be part of the reason why he'd kept his distance this summer? Did he think I liked Tommy back? If Ashlee wasn't in the way on his end, he needed to know that Tommy definitely wasn't on mine.

"Just so you know, dinner is a standing invitation," Tommy said.

Sean glanced across the room at me, and I had no idea what I should say to Tommy.

"I'll keep that in mind," I finally said, distracted by Sean heading back outside, wondering what he might be thinking. I didn't even look fully at Tommy until he slid off my desk.

He rubbed his hands together. "I will break through your defenses and make you mine," he said in a faux-villain sort of way that made me expect him to tack a "bwahaha" on the end. Despite knowing how he might really feel behind his usual teasing, I smiled. I couldn't help it. Tommy really was a funny guy with an infectious personality.

Still, not wanting to encourage him, I stood to add some information to today's trip list on the front counter. Tommy took the opportunity and ran his fingers over the top of my hand and up my bare arm. For a surprising moment, my hormones shoved my real feelings out of the way and I stood motionless, enjoying the sensation of being desired.

I came to my senses and managed to pull away, but not

before Sean reentered the front door and witnessed the intimacy. I jerked away from Tommy, my heart hammering so hard it obstructed part of my hearing.

No, no, no. Why did everything keep going wrong?

Sean made his way over to the gift shop and retrieved a box of granola bars. He placed a five-dollar bill on the counter before leaving—without meeting my eye. My thundering heart sank to my knees. Had I just killed any feelings he might have been developing for me again?

I wanted to scream at my stupidity and ask Sean to forgive me. Instead, I stood frozen and wondered if it was my destiny to spend my life alone. If so, I was going to be so incredibly ticked off, especially if I'd created that destiny by being an idiot.

Tommy glanced at Sean, then winked at me. "See you later."

I said nothing in response.

By the time Sean and then Tommy left the building, all I could do was sink onto the couch and stare at the wall.

The front door opened, but I couldn't find the strength to rise from my seat. Footsteps preceded Mala coming around the corner of the counter before she spotted me and stopped.

I must still look like I'd taken a jolt from a cattle prod, because she asked, "What's wrong?"

It was all I could do to muster the energy to speak. "Tommy just made his feelings known."

"He kissed you?"

"No. He didn't have to."

She shifted her weight to one leg and crossed her arms. "Let me guess. Sean saw?"

I nodded, feeling like my head weighed three times its normal weight.

"Hate to say I told you so."

"I don't need that right now." I let a sigh escape. "How am I going to fix this mess?"

I was asking myself, but Mala answered. "You could use Tommy's crush to make Sean jealous."

I shook my head. "No."

"Why not?"

"No schemes." I caught and held her gaze. "Your half-baked plans never turn out how they're supposed to."

Her expression darkened. "You know what? You can be an ungrateful bitch sometimes."

Her reaction surprised me, but I was unable to think of anything to say before she stalked from the office.

In the first bit of luck I'd had all day, Tommy was talking to Chad down by the river when I closed the office and made my quick getaway. I was even free from chauffeur duty, since Mala had caught a ride back to our grandparents' house with Daniel.

Though I doubted Sean was interested in our little swimming lessons anymore, I drove to the river anyway. If he *was* there, I might die of mortification.

I was truly surprised when I arrived to find him already there. I'd thought meeting him yesterday had been difficult. Ha! Piece of cake compared to today. The scene was pretty much the same when I reached the river, with Sean sitting on the log, waiting for me. However, today it was obvious he wasn't in a good mood.

"You showed up," he said. "Thought you'd be out with Tommy."

He certainly sounded jealous, but it had the opposite effect on me as I'd thought it would. I got mad. If he cared for me, why hadn't he said something? If not, what right did he have to make me feel worse? Boys were such hypocrites!

I crossed my arms and stared hard at him. "You know, sometimes a girl likes to be flirted with, when someone makes her laugh."

"Looks like you've got that covered. First Ian, now Tommy."

"You've got a lot of room to talk after flaunting Ashlee in my face."

He tilted his head slightly. "Ashlee?"

"You do remember Goddess Girl, who couldn't keep her hands off you?"

"Ashlee and I aren't dating. We only went out a couple of times."

The words *went out a couple of times* made me cold all over. I thought I might throw up.

"Could have fooled me." I stripped off my shirt and shorts and strode into the water, letting my anger stampede the panic. I half expected Sean to leave me there alone, but he only hesitated a few seconds before joining me. I was surprised the tension between us didn't congeal the water.

I waded in the shallows until Sean got closer, then stood

to make my way toward the middle of the river. The fear of the watery depths rose in my throat, but I kept swallowing, determined not to look like such a loser in front of Sean. I'd had my fill of that, thanks.

When I felt the rocks and sand beneath my feet start sloping downward, indicating I'd reached the deeper channel of the river, I inhaled a long, deep breath. Then I took a step that was as big to me as Neil Armstrong's was for mankind. Unfortunately, that was when my panic clawed its way to daylight. I flailed when my face went under the water, but somehow my feet found the ground again and my head broke through to fresh air.

Angry and frustrated, I slapped my hands against the surface of the river, splashing water in all directions. "Arrghhhh!" I slapped the water a few more times for good measure.

When water splashed me from the other direction, I looked through my dripping hair to see Sean standing there staring at me. "You splashed me," I said.

"You did it first."

Not knowing what to say, I turned and splashed water in his direction. The next thing I knew, we were in a water fight, splashing with our palms slapping against the surface of the water and scooping handfuls of water at each other.

"Stop it, Sean!" Annoyance filled the air around me.

"You first. You started it."

"Because I almost drowned, you idiot!"

"That's because you were all huffy."

My mouth dropped open. "I'm huffy? Looked in the mirror lately?"

"You're beginning to sound like Mala."

"Oh!" I splashed him extra for that. "Maybe I'm tired of being the responsible one. There's something to be said for having some fun every once in a while."

"I know what you mean," he said as he moved closer before scooping two big handfuls of water at me, hitting me in my shoulder when I turned to shield myself and move into the shallower water.

I screeched, then retaliated.

"You having fun now?" Sean asked as he doused me again, then laughed.

That was when it hit me. Yeah, I was. To get the upper hand, I made an unexpected dive in his direction. He stumbled and fell backward into the water. I hooted and pumped my fists in triumph. But then I gasped when he emerged from the river right in front of me. After he flung the water from his hair, he caught my gaze.

"You win," he said, so softly it felt like a kiss. He lifted his hand and pushed some of my wet hair back off my face.

"Sean." I didn't know what else to say, but I felt compelled to hear his name pass my lips, perhaps asking his lips to come closer.

Something moved, and then I heard a crack in the trees lining the river. Sean heard it too, because he stepped between me and whatever it was. His chivalry made my heart swell, even though I was anxious about whatever had made that noise. We watched and listened for probably a full minute before Sean shook his head.

"It's gone, whatever it was." He reached back to help me from the water. It felt so good to place my hand in his and have him wrap his wonderful fingers around mine.

The small gesture melted whatever frost had still been lingering between us, which made me ridiculously happy.

At least, I was happy until we reached the area where we'd left our clothes on the sandy shore.

They were gone.

CHAPTER 17

I managed to sneak into the house and up to my room without my grandparents noticing that I was only wearing a bathing suit. I was still seriously creeped out that someone had stolen our clothes, which meant someone had been watching us.

By the time I showered and put on a clean outfit, I'd calmed down enough to head downstairs to dinner.

"Where's Mala?" I asked when I saw that the only other people in the kitchen were my grandparents.

"She went over to Parson with Daniel to pick up the new raft we ordered," Grandma said.

I stared at Grandma. "Really?"

She smiled at me as she set a basket of hot rolls on the table. "Yes, dear. Stranger things have happened."

I wondered if she and Daniel might actually act on that spark of attraction I'd seen. Or was Mala just that desperate to steer clear of me?

We'd been sitting at the table less than a minute when Mala clomped in the back door as I scooped mashed potatoes onto my plate. One look at her as she barged into the kitchen made a giant uh-oh zip through my head. She didn't look happy, and I could tell she'd been drinking. Had she and Daniel had a fight?

She looked straight at me, then dropped a gob of wet fabric atop my plate. "You and Sean forgot your clothes."

My heart stopped for a moment before it remembered it had to beat to keep me alive. I noticed Grandma and Grandpa looking at me with shocked expressions.

"It's nothing to get upset over," I said, trying to dispel the images that were likely filling their brains. "We went swimming. Someone stole our clothes from the bank, and now I know who." I gave Mala an angry stare. Not only had she stolen our clothes, but she'd also evidently dunked them in the river.

"Swimming, right," she scoffed. "Looks like Little Miss Perfect isn't so perfect after all. I told everyone not to compare me to her all these years."

It was becoming obvious to my grandparents that Mala was drunk. At least *I'd* never stolen anyone's clothes or come home stinking drunk.

"Mala, have you been drinking?" Grandpa asked. Gone was his normal loving, carefree way of speaking.

She directed her disgusted look at him. "This isn't about me. It's about your goody-goody granddaughter having sex in the woods."

"I didn't have sex in the woods! I wouldn't lie!"

"Oh, right, like you wouldn't lie about your plans for Cooley Mountain Whitewater?"

"Shut up, Mala!"

"No, I won't shut up," she said as she jabbed her forefinger at me. "Has she told you all about how she wants us to sell the business and move away from here? The golden child thinks she knows what's best for everyone."

The look on my grandparents' faces sliced at my heart. "I can explain everything."

"Your dad was right to keep a tight rein on you," Mala said, venom in her voice. "Too bad he went and drowned himself."

Tears flooded into my eyes, and a wave of dizziness slammed into me. I couldn't believe my cousin, whom I loved like a sister, had said such a hateful thing to me about my dad. In front of my grandparents, about their son. What the hell was going on with her?

"Mala!" Grandma jumped from her chair and grabbed Mala's arm. "You will stop this instant."

Mala struggled and yelled, "It's true! She gets away with everything, and everyone thinks I can't do anything right."

I stared at her and wondered what alien had possessed her body. Was it only alcohol talking, or were her true feelings coming out?

Grandma dragged Mala from the room, telling her she didn't know what she was saying, in a harsh voice I'd never heard her use.

I felt like my insides were being shredded, like they had been in the days after my father's broken body washed up onto shore well downstream of Golden Bend. I couldn't relive this, I couldn't! Tears streaked down my face. God, how much more did I have to endure before I'd hit my life-time quota of horribleness?

Grandpa reached over and placed his weather-roughened hand on mine. "I'm so sorry, honey. I don't know what's come over that girl."

I looked up at him and swiped at my tears. "It's not true, not the part about Sean."

"I know." He wasn't offering empty words. He really believed me. Despite how much Mala had hurt me, a twinge of guilt twisted in my gut. I had always been the good one, had rarely gotten in trouble. But was it my fault she'd cho-sen to be more rebellious? Any comparisons were her own fault.

"The other . . . about selling the business." My voice broke. "It was just thoughts." Serious ones, at least for me, but I couldn't handle tackling that topic now, couldn't stand to see any more shock on my grandparents' faces. I wanted to spare everyone more pain, not cause it.

"We don't have to go into that now." I know he was trying to be supportive, but his words made me feel even worse. I felt like I'd betrayed the people who'd always been there for me.

Grandpa continued to try to comfort me, but it didn't do any good. Not only had I lost my father forever, but my mom also might never be the same. And my cousin, my best friend, had resented me for years without me knowing it, so much that she was even making up lies about Dad's death.

I wasn't sure that was something for which I could ever forgive her.

• • •

I lay in bed for hours, staring at the dark rectangle of my window. The tears hadn't lasted long, but the yawning emptiness inside me continued to grow. I suspected it would break through my outer shell soon and consume me like a monster from a science-fiction movie. I felt so sick that I didn't eat my dinner and even refused a slice of cake when Grandma brought it up to me later. All I could think about when I looked at it was that Mala had made it, and that turned my stomach.

I lay in one position so long I began to ache. Some hidden reserve of energy allowed me to sit up on the side of the bed. The house had been quiet for a while now, so I decided to go downstairs and get some lemonade. I might not be hungry, but my throat was as dry as if the Santa Ana winds had been blowing through it.

When I reached the bottom of the stairs, I heard Grandpa talking low. Judging from the lack of a second voice, he must have been on the phone. I wondered if he was telling my aunt and uncle about Mala's display. She thought she'd been punished before. After this, she'd be toast.

"It's time for you to come home," Grandpa said as I peeked around the kitchen doorway. His back was to me, so he didn't notice my presence. "She needs you, Emily."

I retreated from the doorway and closed my eyes as I leaned against the wall. It wasn't one of Mala's parents Grandpa was talking to. It was mine. He meant well, but the last thing I needed right now was to have to deal with my grief-stricken mother.

CHAPTER 18

Over the next couple of days, Mala and I didn't speak, barely made eye contact, and tried not to cross paths more than necessary. I didn't take her to work or give her a lift home. She either rode with Grandma or used one of the company bikes. The guys at work weren't stupid enough to ask what was going on, thank goodness.

I told Sean about the unpleasant scene, and he got upset about Mala's accusation, too. The only good thing to come of the situation was I felt Sean and I were growing closer. When I'd finished telling him about everything Mala had said, he'd wrapped me in his arms and hugged me for a long time. Granted, friends gave the same type of comfort, but this felt more than friendly. Still, I wasn't rushing things. I preferred to let things happen as they happened. No cunning plans, no constantly driving myself insane worrying about whether he didn't like me romantically anymore.

The afternoon two days after the kitchen incident, I ran into Mala as I stepped out the back door. She was climbing the final steps to the back porch, her long hair blowing loose in the warm breeze. When she saw me, she opened her mouth as if to say something. I didn't give her the chance. I turned and retreated back inside, aiming for the front door instead. What had passed between us was going to take a lot more than a simple "I'm sorry" for me to get over it.

Before I reached the front door, however, a man walked in. I glanced back and saw that Mala hadn't followed me inside.

"Can I help you?" I asked as I approached the front counter. The guy looked to be in his early forties, with close-cropped dark hair graying at the temples.

"Yeah, Jack Fraser. My wife and I are booked for a trip this afternoon."

I glanced outside and noticed a blonde woman in a wide-brimmed hat looking up at the trees surrounding the cabin.

Mr. Fraser saw where I was looking. "She's a bird-watcher and spotted some sort of bird up in the trees."

"Ah." I consulted his reservation. "I see you're from Texas. Your first trip to Colorado?"

"Yes," he said as he scanned the photos on the wall depicting years of rafting trips along the Grayton River.

"So what brings you to Golden Bend?" I glanced at him as I asked the question and noticed Grandma coming in the front door.

He cleared his throat. "A friend told me about it, said it was the prettiest place on earth and the rafting the best."

"Your friend was right." After giving him the usual information about the river, safety precautions, and tips on other things to do in the area, I said, "Well, you're all set. If you need anything else, I'm Alex. Just let me know."

He watched me for a long moment. "Alex Landon?"

"Uh, yes." I glanced at Grandma, who was now looking toward us from where she'd been restocking the first-aid cabinet.

He shook his head. "I'm sorry." He looked over at Grandma for a moment, as if he was trying to determine her identity, before turning his attention back to me. "That friend I told you about—it was your dad. I served with him in Iraq."

My entire body clenched. "Oh."

"I was so sorry to hear about his death," he said in a gentle way, as if he was afraid the mention of Dad might make me break into a thousand tiny pieces. He wasn't far off. "My unit was in Iraq until a few weeks ago, so I didn't know until recently."

I had no idea how to respond, so I just stood there looking at him like I was a total dunce. I was vaguely aware of Grandma walking toward me.

"It's nice to meet someone who served with Steve," Grandma said. I could tell she was putting on her Brave Landon Woman face.

Mr. Fraser gave her a small nod and a sad smile. "He was a good man, a good soldier." A pause in conversation hung in the air before Mr. Fraser lifted the brochures I'd given him. "Thank you for these. It was nice to meet you." He turned to leave.

"Mr. Fraser?" Grandma said, causing him to reverse his direction.

"Yes, ma'am?"

"Do you and your wife have dinner plans tonight?"

For a moment, he looked stunned by the question, but he finally answered, "No, not yet."

"Would you consider having dinner with our family?"

No! Please don't do this to me.

I didn't want to be reminded of Dad's time in Iraq, the thing that had changed him so much he'd never recovered. I felt as though one more negative blow would make me irreparable.

"That's kind of you to offer," Mr. Fraser started, sounding as if he were going to decline. Thank goodness.

"Please," Grandma said, evidently sensing the impending refusal as well.

Why was she doing this? Couldn't we leave the past in the past and stop dragging it up, injuring ourselves all over again?

But I didn't voice my objection. I couldn't, not after what Mala had revealed about my plans, ones I still hadn't discussed with my grandparents. They seemed to want to pretend they hadn't heard Mala's accusation, and I was thankful to play along.

"If you're sure."

Grandma nodded, and that was that. I drifted back to my chair while they discussed details, and wondered how I could get out of dinner.

After Mr. and Mrs. Fraser cast off with Sean as their guide, I spent the rest of the afternoon feeling like I needed to go hug the toilet. Instead of working, I mindlessly surfed YouTube. As I shut off the computer at the end of the day, I noticed Mala sitting on one of the benches outside, looking more forlorn than I'd ever seen her. Through the office grape-vine, I'd found out that the night of her drunken tirade she and Daniel had indeed had a fight. I didn't even care what it had been about.

I moved closer to the window, not willing to leave the building until Mala left with Grandma. I noticed she was reading again, a thick book that she didn't even try to hide when the guys rounded the cabin from the river and headed toward their cars. I tracked her line of sight straight to Daniel, who didn't spare her a glance as he said goodbye to Chad and Tommy and got in his car. As he drove away, Mala closed her book and set it on the bench beside her. Now I could see it was *Anna Karenina*.

She looked so incredibly sad and lonely, so unlike herself, that part of me wanted to offer comfort. A very small part.

I waited until Grandma pulled into the parking lot. She'd gone home early to start cooking, but she understood my need to not speak to Mala right now and didn't ask me to bring her home with me.

"Hey, you okay?" Sean asked.

I jumped. "I didn't hear you come in."

"Sorry. I'll try to make more noise next time," he said and smiled.

"You do that," I said, only half paying attention to him.

"You going to be okay tonight?" He'd heard about Mr. Fraser's connection to Dad and the impending dinner while guiding the Frasers downriver.

I took a deep breath. "I guess we'll find out soon enough." Considering I hadn't thought of a way to miss dinner.

When I arrived home, I ran upstairs to change before heading to the kitchen to help Grandma put the finishing touches on our Italian dinner. The scents of garlic and baking bread already filled the air and would have made me hungry if my stomach hadn't been tied in knots.

"Are you upset with me for asking the Frasers to dinner?" she asked me.

I hesitated for a moment before answering. "No, not really."

"You're just nervous?"

I stared out the kitchen window above the sink where I was washing garden-fresh cherry tomatoes for the salad. "More like scared that I won't be able to listen to whatever he says." I took a shaky breath. "I feel like I'm going to crack sometimes."

She gave me a single-armed hug. "It'll be okay. You're a tougher girl than you realize."

I kept forcing that assertion through my mind as Grandpa let the Frasers in the front door and we all sat down to dinner. Well, everyone except Mala. She had to eat her meals in her room.

I picked at my lasagna and garlic bread, too anxious to have much of an appetite. I didn't speak often, but I couldn't help listening, waiting for the bit of information that would make me fall apart. But the conversation centered around the Frasers' life in Texas—he was an engineer for an oil company, she a kindergarten teacher—and what they planned to do while vacationing in Colorado.

The closest we came to talking about Dad was when

Grandpa and Mr. Fraser started comparing rank. Mr. Fraser was a captain, and during Grandpa's stint in the army he'd been a sergeant. Some lighthearted teasing ensued, which only made my nerves tighten more. The longer we didn't talk about Dad, the more desperate to flee I became.

When the remains of the meal were cleared away, I sensed a change in mood and had to force myself not to bolt for the stairs.

"Thank you for inviting us to dinner," Mrs. Fraser said.

"You're more than welcome," Grandma replied.

God, all of this polite small talk was killing me!

I caught Captain Fraser's gaze. "Why did you come here?"

"Alex!" Grandma scolded.

Captain Fraser lifted his hand. "No, it's okay." He looked at me like I was an adult and not a child. Some part of me silently thanked him for that. "Your dad talked about this place so much that I wanted to see it for myself. I thought he had to be exaggerating about it being so beautiful, but he wasn't." He glanced at my grandparents before returning his attention to me. "I'd planned to come up here to go rafting before I heard about your dad. I changed my mind when I found out, but Laura convinced me I should still visit," he said as he squeezed his wife's hand.

"I thought maybe it'd help," Mrs. Fraser said, and that's when I realized: Dad's death had hurt this big, strong man as well.

Captain Fraser cleared his throat. "I felt like I knew all of you, and I admit I was worried about how Steve's death had affected you."

It was a good thing Mom wasn't here for this visit.

"What happened to him?" I asked. "He was so different when he came home." I dreaded the answer but was experiencing the fierce need to know.

Captain Fraser glanced at his wife, who gave him a small nod. He took a deep breath and stared down at the tabletop as he started to talk.

"Our units were assigned to do patrols and guard aid shipments in the little villages around Tikrit. We met a lot of good people whose lives had been turned upside down. Your dad befriended a young girl named Sanaa. She loved hearing about America and about your family and the rafting. She said one day she was going to come here and raft down the river just to see if your dad's stories were true." Mr. Fraser fiddled with his coffee cup for a moment, his expression tight as he dug up memories.

My throat constricted as I suspected this story didn't have a happy ending. "Something happened to her?"

"One day we were watching some little boys playing soccer in this dusty patch beyond the last row of damaged houses in Sanaa's village. Her mother sent her out to get her little brother. We were laughing at Sanaa's efforts to get her brother to stop playing soccer and follow her. She got so frustrated, she said she was going to drag him back by the ear." Captain Fraser paused, swallowed hard. His eyes looked haunted. "When she started forward, she stepped on a hidden land mine. We saw her die."

Oh my God.

"Someone had placed it there since the last time we'd

been in the village, because we'd swept the area and found nothing."

"Why would someone do that?" I asked, my voice shaky with horror.

"Either they thought they'd take out Americans, or it was punishment for the villagers for working with us." Captain Fraser pushed his cup away.

I wondered if he wished he could push away his memories as easily.

"Steve wasn't the same after that," he said. "It was like something broke inside him."

Something I hadn't been able to help him piece back together.

Though it was hard to hear about what had happened to Sanaa and how it'd affected Dad, Captain Fraser's other stories made me proud. Dad was a good-hearted person, so seeing people—even people half a world away—in such horrible situations had gotten to him. But he'd made the best of the situation and used part of his pay to buy everything from food to toys for the people in the villages they'd patrolled. He'd even purchased the soccer ball the little boys had been playing with the day Sanaa had died. Knowing Dad, I understood why it had affected him as it had. That was just too much pain—anguish he would have felt he'd caused.

I wished I'd known the reason behind his brokenness when he'd returned home. Maybe I could have done something to reach him. If he'd been able to talk about Sanaa with me, he might have been able to heal instead of thinking about it all the time. Because I was sure now that memories of what had happened to Sanaa had been occupying his mind the day he went down the river.

After a couple of hours of stories, Captain Fraser—Jack, he insisted we call him—and his wife left to head back to their hotel. They promised to come back sometime to raft again since they'd enjoyed it so much. I didn't reveal that it was possible someone else might own the rafting business by then. Right now, I wasn't sure where I stood on the whole selling-the-business idea.

Grandma kissed me on the forehead before I headed upstairs. Tears glistened in her eyes. I suspected some of them were because she missed Dad, and some were because she was really proud of him and what he'd done for those Iraqi people.

As I climbed the stairs, an overwhelming exhaustion weighed on me. My head was crammed full of images, stories, questions. I wished I could turn off my brain long enough to get a good night of sleep.

When I reached the top of the stairs, a sound made me stop and listen. It was coming from Mala's room. I edged closer and leaned my ear next to the door. She was crying—sobbing, really. My natural instinct to comfort her had me lifting my hand to knock on the door, but then I remembered the spiteful words she'd said about Dad and me. I dropped my hand and stared at the door for a few seconds.

The sound stopped, and I convinced myself I hadn't heard it at all. And if I had, it had been something other than Mala. The wind, maybe, or my imagination. It didn't matter, really, because I wasn't sure I had any forgiveness in me to give. I turned and walked down the hall.

Once inside the four walls of my room, though, I sat on the edge of my bed and wondered what Sanaa would have thought of life in Colorado, a life so much different than the one she'd been handed. Would she have liked river rafting? The mountains? The freedom? The not worrying that she might be killed by some crazy-ass dictator every day?

Everything I had and took for granted.

A light knock sounded on my door. "Alex?" said Mala from the other side, her voice muffled.

I stared at the inside of my door but didn't answer. When she said my name again, I lay down on my side and pulled my pillow over my head, shutting out the sound of Mala's voice.

And the rest of the world.

CHAPTER 19

The next morning, I got to work late because of an early dental appointment. When I arrived, the office was empty. I knew the guys were out on rafting trips, but Mala and my grandparents were nowhere to be seen. I rounded the counter and noticed a heaping plate of cookies atop the desk. I always seemed to want something sweet after going to the dentist, as if gobs of sugar were okay, since my teeth were squeaky-clean.

I lifted the cling wrap and grabbed a cookie. Oatmeal chocolate chip—my favorite. As I bit into the delicious cookie, I wandered to the back door and glanced outside. Mala sat halfway down the steps, the portable phone and appointment book beside her. I glanced back at the cookies, realizing she'd made them as a peace offering. As I'd told Tommy at the drive-in, I ate when I was upset. When Mala was upset, she baked.

How was I supposed to feel about her gesture? Appreciate the fact she knew she'd messed up? Or maintain my anger because Mala hadn't come groveling with her apology?

I leaned my shoulder against the door frame and watched

my cousin stare at the river. I was glad for the lack of Mala antics the past few days, but at the same time, I missed her hard-to-contain bubbliness. It was almost as if she wasn't the real Mala anymore. There had to be a happy medium between out-of-control Mala and the shell of her real self sitting out there, right?

I turned my gaze to the river too. Since our last swimming excursion, I'd had zippo time alone with Sean other than the brief moment yesterday afternoon before I'd had to go home and have dinner with the Frasers. Not exactly the right moment to dive into a much-needed conversation. The frustration rose in me at not having the opportunity I needed, especially now that I thought I might still have a chance to be with Sean.

I wandered back to my desk but found concentrating on work impossible. Instead, I let scenarios for talking to Sean run through my mind as I piddled with my Facebook account. I needed to get everything out in the open between us. I'd skirted around the issue long enough. The weeks of summer were passing by, and before I knew it, Sean would be headed back to Denver.

Even with my new resolve, I couldn't banish the butterflies in my stomach. Self-doubts plagued me, though I knew I'd seen signs that Sean still liked me. Hadn't I?

The back door opened. I closed the Facebook page and opened a Quicken file on the computer to make myself look busy.

Mala placed the phone back in its charger and returned the appointment book to the edge of the desk, all without a word. She walked past me and headed toward the gift shop side of the building.

How long was I willing to keep up the cold war between us? Without Mala to talk to, I felt even lonelier than usual.

"Thanks for the cookies," I said.

She looked back at me with her mouth partially open, as if she didn't know how to respond. "I knew you'd want something sweet this morning."

All was not healed, but at least we'd both taken tentative steps in the ways we knew how.

A half hour later, the guys streamed through the back door after a large outing with a group of Boy Scouts that had required all of them.

Chad and Daniel sank onto the couch while Sean and Tommy made a beeline for the fridge to quench their thirsts.

"Remind me why I do this again," Chad said.

"Because the other option requires you to say, 'Would you like fries with that?' and an ugly uniform," Sean answered as he walked back with a soda for him and two more for the couch sitters.

"What we need is a party," Tommy said as he parked himself on the end of my desk again. "Is the barn blowout still on?"

Everyone looked at me, and I responded by sitting there like the definition of "inert."

"Definitely," Mala said, sounding more like her old self.

I stared at her, and she gave me a forced smile. "Tommy's right. We need something fun to do." The expression on her face as she looked at me was half apologetic, half challenging. Was she testing me to see if I would go along or play Miss Goody Two Shoes again?

When I looked back at the guys, they were still watching me, waiting for my seal of approval. "I guess so."

Sean smiled at me in a way that made me glad the party was still taking place. Call it gut instinct.

"The sooner the better," Tommy said.

"This weekend sounds great," Mala said as she moved closer to the rest of the group.

"As long as we keep it under wraps," I said. "Our grandparents can't find out." Not after the week they'd had—and not on the heels of Mala's accusation against Sean and me and the resulting fallout. My grandparents trusted me, and I wanted to keep it that way.

"Got it," Tommy said.

"We'll need to clean out the barn," Mala said. "It's full of old junk."

"I'm free tonight," Daniel said.

If I hadn't seen the spark between them that night at the river, I likely wouldn't have noticed the quick glance he shot Mala as anything out of the ordinary. But I had seen that spark, and if I wasn't mistaken, Mala's cheeks had just grown a little pinker.

The rest of the guys chimed in that they'd be able to help as well.

"Okay, we'll meet around eight." I gave directions on how to reach the barn without passing my grandparents' house.

When the guys filed back out the door to prep for the

next raft trip, Mala started rearranging a display of foam soda can holders that didn't need to be straightened.

"Why?"

Mala didn't pretend to not know what I meant.

"Just what I said. I think everyone needs something fun to do." She glanced at me, then focused on the can holders.

I suspected there was more to her motives, but I didn't push the topic.

The rest of the day went by quickly and slowly at the same time. Quickly because our busy stream of vacationers escaping the heat of lower elevations didn't show any sign of stopping. Slowly because I kept wondering if tonight was the night I'd find the opportunity to spill everything to Sean and hope for the best.

Things were still a little tense between Mala and me as I drove us home.

"I guess we can just tell Grandma and Grandpa that we're going to go for a walk after dinner," I said as I pulled into the ranch's driveway.

"*You're* going for a walk. I'm grounded, remember?"

I balked a bit at the bitterness in her voice. She'd brought her punishment on herself, after all. But I forced myself not to say what I was thinking.

"Why didn't you say something earlier?"

She shrugged as I parked. "No biggie. Can't say I'll miss moving a bunch of old junk anyway."

Mala started to get out of the car, but I placed my hand on her forearm to stop her. "What about the party?"

"There will be plenty of other parties," she said in a flip

way I didn't quite believe. "Plus, I see you people all day every day. I think I'll spend some quality time with Jensen Ackles on DVD."

I nearly asked her about Daniel, but she slipped out of the car and hurried toward the house.

When I climbed the stairs to my room, Mala's door was shut, and all was silent on the other side. I wondered if she'd closed me out so she could let her façade dissolve. With a sigh, I retreated to my room to change clothes and check my e-mail. To my surprise, there was one from Sean.

"Hey. Can't bring the sound system tonight without Dad seeing and asking unwanted questions. Chad bringing radio instead. Later, Sean."

I responded with a simple "okay" even though I was tempted to just pour out all of my feelings in an e-mail. It'd be so much easier, and the rejection less mortifying if I received it in the privacy of my own room. Plus, there was the bonus of my bed being right next to my desk. Easy access if the need to curl into the fetal position and cry myself to sleep arose.

After shutting off my computer, I headed downstairs to eat, even though I was so nervous I doubted I could consume much. Mala's door was open now, in anticipation of Grandma bringing her dinner up to her. I glanced in and noticed Mala reading again. I stepped into the doorway and saw the title—*Pride and Prejudice.*

"Since when did you become Queen of the Classics?"

"Since I got grounded. I can only stare at these four walls for so long before I go completely whacked."

I crossed my arms and shook my head. "It's obvious you

and Daniel like each other. But you're both too stubborn to admit it."

"Just because I've decided to broaden my literary horizons does not mean I like Book Boy."

"No, but I've seen the looks you send his direction when he isn't watching."

She placed the book in her lap and opened her mouth as if to argue, but then closed it. "Even if I did like him, it wouldn't matter."

"Why not?"

"Because I'm not his type of girl."

"The looks *he* sends *you* say otherwise."

Her head whipped toward me before she could hide her surprise. "He's probably just wondering what idiotic thing I'm going to do next."

"Trust me, that's *not* the kind of look he's giving you."

"If you're saying that to punish me, it's cruel."

I stiffened at the accusation. "I'm not."

I turned and headed down the stairs, leaving Mala to mull over my parting words.

Dinner with my grandparents seemed to take about three years, but when I was finally free I hesitated and looked at the stairs. I wondered—would Mala and I ever be close again, or would we just keep piling hurt on top of hurt?

Okay, so she wasn't perfect. But in the absence of siblings, she was all I had.

"Grandma?"

"Yes, dear?" Grandma said from where she stood at the sink running hot water for the dishes.

"Can Mala go with me for a walk?"

"Are you sure you want to do that?"

"Yeah." I didn't elaborate, but Grandma nodded.

I climbed the stairs and knocked on Mala's door before poking my head in. "Come on. We're going for a *walk*."

She didn't question her sudden freedom, but jumped from the bed and followed me downstairs and out the back door.

"How'd you manage to spring me?"

"I just asked."

"Golden Child strikes again."

"Don't call me that." My words hit the air with such a chill that even Mala winced.

"Okay."

We tried to look casual and not in a hurry as we strolled down the lane that led to the back of our grandparents' property. Only when we passed out of sight of the house did we abandon the pretense and start running through the slanting rays of the setting sun. By the time we reached the barn, we were gasping. The guys, who were sitting on hay bales inside, looked at us like we were the silliest things they'd ever encountered.

The scent of pine and tall grass was thick on the cooling air. It was replaced when we entered the barn, however, by those of dusty hay and old oily machinery. My nose twitched in response. But the place had potential.

I scanned the interior, refamiliarizing myself with the layout. A wide-open area straight through the length of the barn was flanked by a couple of horse stalls and a tack room toward the back. The rest of the lower level and the two sides of the loft overlooking the open middle held bales of hay and forgotten machines.

"We don't have much time, so let's get to it," I said. "Chad and Tommy, start moving all the old hay bales up against the walls for seats. Daniel, help Mala scoop up the loose hay and toss it into one of the old barrels out back."

Mala shot me a look like I'd thrown her in a cage with a hungry tiger, but I ignored her.

"What about me?" Sean asked. I was so far gone for him that even that simple question sounded sexy.

"I could use some help moving the hay bales in the loft."

Chad snickered, and I shot him a "shut up or die" look. Tommy didn't look as amused, but I did my best to ignore that as well. The sooner he got the point that I wasn't interested in him, the better. When he started goofing off with Chad, I began to think I'd been worrying for no reason.

"Ugh, you're getting dust all over me!" Mala squealed at Daniel.

"You're in the way."

I rolled my eyes and headed for the ladder to the loft. Sean and I climbed to the upper level with the intent of rearranging hay bales for party guests to sit on and talk out of the way of the dancing. When I found myself right above Mala and Daniel, I smiled. I scooped up a handful of loose hay, walked to the edge of the loft as easily as I could so the floorboards didn't creak, and dropped it right on their heads.

"Wha—?" Mala shrieked as she jumped and started

knocking hay from her hair and shoulders, squealing like I'd poured some of Tommy's green goo hangover cure atop her head.

I laughed at her "I'm so a girl" moment.

She looked up with payback in her eyes. "You're going to regret that," she said.

"I'm so scared," I responded as I returned to my original task.

"But you look so lovely as a scarecrow," Tommy said to Mala, earning him a bunch of hay in the face.

As we all continued rearranging hay bales, shoving old junk into the corners, and planning where the refreshment tables and music setup would go, jokes flew across the barn, including many of the "roll in the hay" variety. Tommy invited me to go for said roll, but I declined and tried to make sure I didn't find myself alone with him.

I thought I saw him look annoyed at my giving him the cold shoulder, but since he was flirting with Mala too I tried to convince myself that I didn't have anything to worry about. If there had been more girls there, Tommy would have been flirting with them too. He wasn't a one-girl kind of guy, his advances to the contrary.

Besides, my attention was focused much more on another guy in my vicinity. Several times I looked across the barn to see Sean watching me. My skin warmed each time, and excited jitters danced across my skin. I believed we were on the verge of something, not like anything we'd shared before. Maybe too much had happened between us and to us since we'd been together the first time. Maybe it wouldn't be the same this time around, but I got all giddy thinking that it could be . . . *better*.

When I started to drag a piece of machinery I couldn't even identify out the back of the barn, Sean sprang to help lift part of the load. I smiled at him, and I suspected all of my feelings about him were revealed in that smile. Well, good. Now I wouldn't have to figure out how to actually put those feelings into coherent words, right?

As I backed out of the barn and made the turn to place the equipment against the back wall, I tripped on an old tire. My hands slipped off the machinery as I tried to catch myself. No such luck. I ended up on my butt in the grass. Nice.

Sean dropped his end of the metal contraption and rushed to my side. He stooped beside me. "Are you okay?"

I am now, I thought as I looked up into his eyes so close. "Fine. Just showing off my klutzy side."

"You're sure?" Sean's eyes didn't leave mine. Was it my imagination, or did he sound a little breathless?

I couldn't answer. The only thing I could think was, *Kiss me!* As if he heard my thoughts, he lifted his hand to the side of my face, caressed my cheek with his thumb, and leaned in. *Yes!*

"Hey, no sitting down on the job," Tommy said, totally breaking the moment. I wanted to scream and kick him all the way back to England.

"You are this close," I said, holding my thumb and

forefinger half an inch apart, "to me calling INS and swearing up and down you're an illegal alien." I said it sarcastically, but I did wish he'd suddenly disappear.

Sean gave me what looked like a "later" expression, a promise, before helping me to my feet. As I dusted off the back of my shorts, someone inside turned on the radio Chad had brought to check out the sound in the barn. Tommy grabbed my hand and pulled me inside.

"We've got to test the dance floor, right?" he asked as he pulled me into the open area in the middle of the barn and spun me in a circle.

If Tommy tried to kiss me again, I swore I *would* kick him. I imagined Sean breaking in like guys always did in romantic movies. Instead, as Tommy guided me around and around, I noticed Sean leaning against one of the roof supports, watching me and smiling. There was a lot behind that smile, and my heart beat faster than even the dancing could account for.

CHAPTER 20

Despite my agreement that the party could take place, my old anxieties returned as Mala and I got ready on party day. We were already deceiving our grandparents by getting ready at her house. Why couldn't I simply enjoy myself without thinking something would go wrong?

Mala stopped fixing my hair and met my eyes in the full-length mirror hanging on her closet door. "Stop worrying."

"I'm not." I fidgeted in the desk chair she had placed in front of the mirror.

"You are. You're getting the scrunchy marks here." She pointed to my forehead with a newly painted nail. How did she keep her nails so nice anyway? I was forever chipping or breaking mine at work.

"Fine, so I'm a wee bit anxious."

"It's only because you're going to tell Sean how you feel about him tonight, even if I have to tie the both of you to a tree and leave you there until you admit your feelings for each other."

"Okay, drastic much?" It felt good to be slowly mending our relationship.

"I do what has to be done," Mala said in a mock martyr voice that had me rolling my eyes.

When we finished getting ready, I considered my reflection in the mirror. The girl who stared back looked like me, and yet she didn't. Gone were my normal cute sporty clothes like capri pants with a baby-doll tee or a tennis mini with a V-neck tee. In their place, I was wearing a little red dress that fell in soft folds to right above my knees. A new strapless bra created the illusion that I had more cleavage than I did. My wavy, dark brown hair was full of all the body that today's plethora of hair products could produce. I was happy with the results. I hoped Sean would be too.

Mala, freed from her grounding when she was with me, drove to the back entrance to our grandparents' property, a partially overgrown roadway that hadn't been used much during my lifetime. It was where we'd instructed all of the invitees to park, out of sight of the main road.

"Um, why are there like a million cars here?" I asked Mala as I glanced over at her, my anxiety building.

She shrugged. "Don't look at me. I don't know."

We trekked the rest of the way on foot. We couldn't have gotten closer to the barn in the car if we'd wanted to. When I stepped in the front door, my mouth fell open. Not an attractive look. But what was I supposed to do when I saw roughly half of our school inside, not to mention many people I didn't even recognize?

Tommy made his way through the crowd with two plastic cups of beer from the enormous keg. He looked summery and ready to party in white cargo shorts and a sea foam green casual button-down. I doubted he'd be alone much tonight.

"Glad you could make it, ladies," he said as he extended the cups to us.

I took one and swallowed a drink, hoping it would help calm me down. It didn't. This party had "disaster" written all over it. "Where did all these people come from?"

"Oh, word got out. Not much else happening around here, you know."

"Exactly *how* did word get out?"

He smiled at me, totally unconcerned by my nervousness about the potential for Coloradans Gone Wild on my grand-parents' back acreage. "I might have told a few people."

"By people, you mean girls," Mala said.

A strange look passed over Tommy's face, a brief moment of annoyance. What did he have to be annoyed about? He had a girl smorgasbord and enough beer to soak the U.S. Army. When my eyes met his, the intensity there made me look away. If I didn't acknowledge his attraction, it'd cease to exist. At least, I kept telling myself that.

Daniel pushed his way through the crowd, wearing loose, trendy jeans and a bright blue tee. And I'd have sworn he looked like he'd taken more care with his hair. As in, he'd done more than run his fingers through it. He spotted Mala, and looked like he might drool on himself as his gaze traveled over her. "You look great," he said.

"Uh, thanks," Mala replied, sounding flustered.

I stared in awe. Mala *never* sounded flustered.

Daniel shifted on his feet and looked back through the crowd as though he wanted to make a quick getaway.

"Oh, for heaven's sake, will you two go dance?" I said as I shoved Mala toward Daniel.

Mala tripped over her own feet and right into Daniel. He grabbed her arms and steadied her. There it was again, that spark of attraction when they were close to each other, the spark both of them had been fighting against. But this time, they didn't move away from each other. Instead, Daniel took Mala's hand and pulled her toward the dance floor, leaving me with Tommy. Great, I'd just match-made my way into an uncomfortable situation.

Tommy tossed his beer aside and guided me toward the midst of the dancing too, and I was too stunned by everything around me to protest. When his hands drifted too low on my back, however, I did give him a "not one inch lower" look.

"Come on, loosen up," he said. "We're here to have a good time."

I did want to have this party. I wanted it to lift me out of the funk caused by the stories of Dad's time in Iraq and the fresh wave of missing him and how things used to be. As the song ended, I felt a hand at my elbow and turned to see Sean there. My breath hitched halfway up my throat. He wore khakis and a blue button-down shirt, which went great with his dark eyes and summer-lightened hair. Oh my, he looked so good in blue. How could I have forgotten that?

My heart rate kicked up a notch, and a wide smile took up residence on my face. Sean looked great all the time, but when he dressed up a little . . . I resisted the need to fan myself.

It was on the tip of my tongue to tell him how wonderful he looked, to just blurt out how he made my heart want to explode with love and longing. But he spoke first instead.

"Can I have the next dance?"

"Sure." I really hoped my answer didn't sound as breathless as I thought it did.

"Yeah, well, I'll catch you later," Tommy said as he stepped back. "Got to share myself, love."

I glanced at Tommy as he disappeared into the crowd. While he was trying to appear like his carefree, hopeless flirt self, I saw that it was all a front. Guilt pecked at me, but it wasn't my fault who he liked. And I'd done nothing to encourage him. When Sean pulled me close for the next song, however, I forgot about everything but how warm and solid and fantastic he felt pressed next to me. I looked up into his eyes and saw him watching me like he wished we were alone.

Part of me cheered while another part totally freaked out. I tried to calm the freaked-out part by laying my head against his chest, closing my eyes, and moving to the music. This felt wonderful.

I had to calm down before I could talk to him coherently. This conversation had to go just right, and that wasn't going to be possible if I began babbling like an idiot. But waiting even a minute more was killing me!

Every touch and movement sent prickles of awareness racing over my skin and did little to calm my crazed heartbeat. His hand moving up my back. The sway of our bodies against each other. His breath against my hair. I soaked it all in and chose to let my anxiety about the party go. It was likely all for nothing anyway.

When his mouth moved close to my ear, every nerve ending in my body fired simultaneously. If we'd been standing in the dark instead of a barn lit by three bay lights hanging from the roof beams, I suspected I'd have been glowing.

"You look beautiful," he said, barely audible over the ballad playing on his new radio.

I smiled against his chest before lifting my gaze to his. We stared at each other for what felt like forever. Dozens of people surrounded us, but they might as well have been floating around on Saturn's rings. My heart beat at an insane rate as Sean bent toward me. *Please, please don't let anyone interrupt.*

No one did. I'd kissed Sean before, but even our first kiss paled in comparison. Happiness welled inside me, threatening to burst forth like the rays of the sun. But that happiness mixed with nervousness that some other obstacle was going to reveal itself.

He guided my head back against his chest. I felt intensely alive, but the little doubt demons whispered in my ear, asking why he'd stopped with one kiss. Was that it? Would there be no more? Had my kiss not lived up to Ashlee's?

Once my own pulse quieted a little, I heard his faster-than-normal heartbeat against my ear. That was a good thing, right?

Stop it! As if my life didn't throw enough trouble at me, I had to seek out more. I just needed to enjoy the fact that

Sean was holding me again, that he'd *kissed* me. That maybe he still wanted me.

If I ignored the concerns I'd shoved aside, I had to admit this night was absolutely perfect. Even if my grandparents busted us within the next minute, it would have been worth it.

I have no idea how many songs we danced to before Mala pulled me away. Once we were in a less-crowded corner, she did a little happy dance.

"Things seem to be going well. I will refrain from saying, 'I told you so.'"

I glanced back toward the refreshment table, where Sean stood getting a drink and talking to Daniel. "I haven't felt this good in a long, long time." I eyed the guys a moment longer before looking back at Mala. She was watching Daniel with a dreamy expression on her face, one I'd never seen before. "You really like him, don't you?"

"Yes." She didn't even hesitate in answering. "He's like no one I've ever dated. Guess that shows I've been dating the wrong guys." She looked back at me. "I can't describe how I feel. It's all so jittery and silly and like I might start floating at any minute."

"I think I have an idea." When I looked across the barn this time, Sean met my gaze. Yes, I knew exactly how Mala felt. I was pretty sure my feet were beginning to lift off the floor as unspoken feelings passed between Sean and me. Amazing, the power of simple eye contact.

After our little chat, Mala grabbed Sean and pulled him toward the dance floor. One of her loving-life laughs drifted above the sounds of "Wings of a Butterfly" by HIM—one of the European bands Tommy had been introducing us to all summer. Feeling equally as happy, I commandeered Daniel, who looked startled.

"Hey, she steals my guy, I steal hers," I said to him.

With a shrug, he dropped all protest he might have uttered. I thought Mala and Daniel, as different as they were, might be good for each other.

HIM's song flowed into various American pop songs and then into Lacuna Coil's "Closer"—another of Tommy's contributions. We all kept switching dance partners and comparing notes on the pluses and minuses of each partner, causing laughter and mock outrage.

At one switch-off, I found myself back in front of Sean. The hilarity changed to heightened awareness. My skin crackled with static electricity.

"Nope, my turn," Tommy said as he stepped between us and grabbed my hand too tightly.

I jerked my hand out of his, which caused him to face me. Ugh. His breath told me he'd been drinking too much. As if his sudden change in personality hadn't given me a clue.

"Ah, come on, Boss Lady," he said. "You've danced with everyone else."

"I danced with you first, Tommy. Of course, you're so schnockered you probably don't remember."

Tommy took a step forward and pulled me to him.

"Stop it!" I pushed against his chest.

Sean jerked Tommy free of me and forced him away so

hard he stumbled and nearly fell backward. "She said no," he bit out, obviously holding even more back.

Tommy's face went red, and he retaliated by slapping his hands against Sean's chest and pushing him back a couple of steps. "Shove off! You've had your turn." He looked at Sean with a hard stare and his nostrils flaring, like he wanted to beat the crap out of him. In his present state, I didn't give Tommy good odds on that count. Not to mention Sean was taller and a few pounds heavier than him.

"Move away," Sean said in a none-too-friendly voice.

"Bite me."

Wow, the testosterone and animosity building around us could have blown the barn apart at the seams. I'd felt the occasional friction between Sean and Tommy ever since the river incident with the floating hat, which had been made worse by the move Tommy had made on me in the office. I'd thought they were past it, but evidently not. I had to get them away from each other before this really fun party turned into a really ugly brawl. Brawls never turned out well for anyone.

Sean made a threatening move toward Tommy, but I stepped between them and placed my hand against the front of Sean's shirt.

Tommy laughed. "Need a girl to fight for you, pretty boy?"

Sean growled and tried to get past me again, but I shoved against him enough that he stopped. Then I whirled on Tommy.

"You're making an ass of yourself. Either you cool it, or you can go home."

He snorted in disgust, and an ugly sneer transformed his normally handsome face. "I thought you were different, but you're as big a whore as your cousin."

CHAPTER 21

I felt as if Tommy had slapped me with those words. This time, I didn't try to hold back Sean as he roared and launched himself at Tommy. I was too stunned to move.

Sean tackled Tommy and threw a couple of punches before Chad and Daniel were able to drag him off our Jekyll-and-Hyde coworker. Sean struggled against them, but Chad used his larger bulk to drag him back a few feet. When Tommy tried to launch a counterattack, Daniel displayed strength I didn't know he had and shoved Tommy back.

"Get the hell out of here or I'll punch you myself."

Tommy smacked Daniel's hand away but thankfully took a couple of steps back. "Gladly. This is a bloody stupid party anyway." He made his way through the crowd, which began to filter back onto the floor space that had opened up for the fight. Conversations started again. Couples drifted back into dancing to the music while casting curious glances at those of us involved in the altercation.

Daniel stepped forward and put his arm around Mala. "Come on," she said with forced brightness, ignoring the fact that Tommy had called her a whore in front of probably fifty people. "It's still a party, and we're here to have fun."

Anger radiated off Sean like heat as he stared at the open doorway on the opposite side of the barn through which Tommy had retreated.

Sean's hand wrapped around mine. "Let's get out of here." He guided me through the crowd toward the matching open doorway at the back of the barn and out into the night. We headed toward the dark woods lining the river. I didn't ask why, simply walked alongside him and let the music and light fade as we left them and everyone else behind.

The anger still pulsed in him, and I gently squeezed his hand. "It's over now. He's gone. He'll go sleep it off and hopefully not be such a raving jerk tomorrow."

"I knew he liked you, but I thought it was harmless." He stopped and looked down at me. "I'm sorry."

I ran my thumb over the back of his hand. "It's not your fault. I didn't see that coming either."

Sean let out a breath and stared up at the sky, at the dark clouds drifting past the moon. "I'd feel better if I'd gotten in one good punch to his stupid mouth."

We'd been having such a nice time before Tommy had gone mental. I wanted to recapture that closeness with Sean, to make the thoughts of Tommy go away. I tugged on Sean's hand and started leading him toward the forest again.

Once we began weaving through the trees, I remembered the old fort. "Hey, I want to show you something." Though dark clouds kept blowing past it, the moon gave me enough light to find the spot I sought.

"Do you remember this place?"

"It's where we built the fort that summer."

My eyes widened. "I'm surprised you remember."

"Why would you be? You remembered, didn't you?"

"Yes, but—"

He took a step closer and pulled me to within an inch of him. "But guys don't remember those kinds of things, right?"

"No, not typically," I said, teasing him to hide my nervousness.

He ran his fingertips across my cheek and down my jaw before lifting my face so that he could kiss me. He kissed me in the moonlight at the spot where I'd first known I'd loved him. Yes, I'd known even then.

"I remember lots of things," he said as his lips lifted from mine.

"Like?"

"How much I like kissing you."

"The feeling's mutual." I smiled, and he smiled back. The smiles gave way to another kiss.

When we separated, an unwanted thought entered my head. I realized I had to risk ruining the evening by asking a question. "There's really nothing between you and Ashlee?"

He didn't pretend ignorance. "It was only a couple of dates. I told you that."

"Seemed like more than that to her."

"Yeah, but I told her I wasn't interested before she went back to Denver."

"Really?"

He pulled me closer. "Really." And then he kissed me again, longer and slower than the previous kisses.

After he lifted his lips from mine, I leaned back enough to look into his eyes. "Do you remember the time capsule?"

He looked confused for a moment before the memory surfaced. "Yeah."

"How about where we buried it?"

He took a step back and looked around me at the small clearing amongst the trees. "Not sure. I think so."

"I thought it might be fun to find it."

At first, I thought he was going to disagree, but then he walked around me. "Be easier with a shovel, but a stick should do."

I joined the search for a sturdy stick, but Sean found one before I'd barely taken half a dozen steps in my cute silver sandals. I wasn't exactly wearing the best in hiking attire— something I'd teased Mala about on many occasions.

Sean dug for about ten minutes in a total of three different spots before his stick made a thunking, wood-hitting-plastic sound. I hurried to his side to watch as he finished uncovering the familiar Spider-Man lunchbox.

With Spidey recovered from the forest floor, we sank onto a log where the moon shone down, illuminating our find.

"Wow, seems like just yesterday we buried that," I said. "But it seems like a long time ago, too."

"Yeah." Sean looked over at me with his hand resting near the opening clasp of the lunchbox. "You ready?"

I nodded, trying to remember what all I'd put inside the

time capsule. When he opened the lid, however, I started laughing.

"What?"

I reached into the box and pulled out the Snickers bar that had been one of Sean's contributions. There had been a time when he'd eaten at least one Snickers every day. I turned it so I could see where he'd used a black marker to write, *the best candy bar ever*, along the side of the wrapper, barely visible now in the near darkness.

"I'm sure this is tasty now. Not positive future excavators would agree with your candy critique."

"I bet it's so full of preservatives it's still good."

"Eew." I tossed the candy bar to the side.

We sifted through the newspaper clippings, movie ticket stubs, a brochure for Cooley Mountain Whitewater, and other assorted things that had been deemed important by our younger selves.

"Ah, here's a gem," Sean said as he held up a small photo to the light. "Frilly."

I grabbed the photo. Ugh. It was the one in which Mom had made me wear a pink top with ruffly sleeves. "Bleh. This should be burned so it doesn't put out anyone's eyes."

Sean took it back from me. "What? You were cute."

"Uh, yeah, right."

"You were. Still are." He leaned over and gave me a quick kiss.

After we stared at each other for a moment, I took the lunchbox from him and dug through the last few items. I found his corresponding school photo and laughed. "Look at that. Your mama dressed you funny too."

"I don't know what you're talking about. Checked shirts were the height of fashion."

I snorted, but in my mind I remembered how much I'd treasured my own copy of this photo once my feelings for Sean had changed that summer. Of course, I hadn't said anything to him.

He hadn't looked at me any differently until last summer when he'd come to my rescue after I'd had a flat tire in the pouring rain. Combining our strength, we'd managed to get it changed, even though we got soaked to the bone. He looked up at me after he placed the last lug nut on, saw I was shivering, and pulled me to him. We'd hugged before, as friends. But something had changed with that hug—a new awareness blossomed. And Sean had kissed me for the first time.

I stared into the bottom of the lunchbox, and only our two secret items remained, both wrapped to hide their identity. Before I could reach inside, however, Sean grabbed his and stuffed it in his pocket.

"Hey, that's not fair!"

"It's a secret."

"Yeah, when we were ten. What's the big secret now?"

"It just is."

My curiosity shot sky-high. I reached for the hidden item.

"Oh, no, you don't," he said, and turned to make his pocket inaccessible.

Undeterred, I tried to get at it from the other side. We went back and forth like this, laughing, wrestling, until I ended up on Sean's lap, one leg on either side of him. I stopped and stared into his eyes. There was no disguising how Sean was reacting to the position. My breath felt trapped in my lungs, and my heart was pounding hard against my chest. My skin warmed. I started to move off him, but he placed his hands on my bare arms.

"No, don't," he said, his voice different, lower and husky sounding.

He slid his hand up through my hair and splayed his fingers at the back of my head, pulled me down so that our lips met. The kisses were different too, faster, more desperate.

Sean pulled away and leaned his forehead against my chest. His warm breath drifted across my chest, making my skin tingle.

"We need to go back," he said, his voice thick and full of the fact that it was the last thing he wanted to do.

But neither of us moved. He lifted his mouth to mine again, and I poured all my yearning and love into kissing him.

Sean slid off the back of the log to lie in the grassy area behind it. He looked into my eyes and caressed my cheek. "You're beautiful." He pulled me so close I forgot how to breathe, forgot about the world outside this patch of moonlit clearing.

I stared up at the inky blackness of the sky as I lay next to Sean some time later. The moon and stars had been totally covered by clouds now, but I still thought it the most beautiful night ever.

I'd thought I knew about sex. I mean, I'd taken sex ed, read love scenes in novels, even seen sex scenes in movies. But nothing had prepared me for how strange and yet wonderful it was when you shared it with someone you loved. I was so happy, I was afraid my smile might break my face.

I pushed away the feeling of impending doom that was trying to rob me of my happiness. Nothing would ruin our relationship this time.

I knew lots of people who were no longer even with the girl or guy they'd lost their virginity to. Some gave in to peer pressure, others to curiosity. I'd always had in my mind that Sean would be my first, and I was glad I'd waited. We weren't like the others. We'd make it.

"You cold?" Sean asked as he rubbed his hand up and down my arm.

We still lay in the clearing, though the cool night air had necessitated us putting our clothes back on. At least Sean's shirt was still open, and I lazily ran my fingertips over his warm skin.

"No. I'm fine."

He tipped my head up and kissed me with such gentleness, sweetness. "You are much more than fine."

I smiled like a fool. Any girl would have if she felt this incredibly happy. It was like Sean had thawed the frozen crust that had been surrounding my heart since Dad's death and our breakup.

"So are you," I said as I placed my head on his chest. "I

don't ever want to leave here." I hoped the admission didn't freak him out.

After a few seconds, he stroked the hair on my head and said, "Me neither."

We didn't talk about what would happen next, and I wasn't brave enough to bring it up. We were closer than we'd ever been, and I was satisfied to let things progress at their own pace. I wouldn't risk losing him again.

The explorations of my fingers seemed to arouse Sean again, and we started kissing.

I was the first to notice sounds that shouldn't have been invading our little paradise. "What's that?"

Sean lifted his head and listened. Cleared of the fog of desire, we both realized what was drifting through the trees toward us. Sirens. Screams.

I turned my head and looked through the darkness back toward the barn. A faint orange glow lit the horizon. "Oh God!"

We both jumped to our feet and started running, Sean with his open shirt flying back behind him and me leaving my shoes beside the log. My heart beat like crazy with exertion and fear. As we emerged from the woods, I skidded to a stop and stared in horror at the flames licking the old wood of the barn.

The disaster I'd feared had found us.

CHAPTER 22

Horror surged through me as I stared at the flames licking the sides of the barn like a hungry demon. I could feel the heat from where I stood frozen at the edge of the woods. Fear tunneled into me with razor-sharp claws, making me imagine the worst possible scenario—people trapped inside. Party guests were running everywhere, some of them nothing but frantic silhouettes against the roaring blaze. A fire truck rolled up to the barn, and police officers were grabbing teenagers and gesturing toward the burning structure.

Oh God, please don't let anyone still be inside.

The wind shifted, sending smoke in our direction. I coughed and brought my hand up to my mouth. The bright orange of the flames and the strobing red lights atop the fire truck made me dizzy and caused me to stumble forward several steps. Those first steps propelled me toward the barn. My friends were in there.

Sean grabbed my arm, bringing me out of my daze. I tried to free myself, but he held firm.

"I've got to help them!"

Movement out of the corner of my eye drew my attention.

A sheriff's deputy headed toward us, his face set in determined lines until a couple of people fleeing the barn ran right into him, causing them all to topple over onto the ground.

"Come on," Sean said as he dragged me away from the barn. "We've got to get out of here."

Still, I balked, dug in my heels. "But Mala?" Why had we fought? Was I being punished again? I couldn't lose someone else I loved.

Sean gripped the upper part of both of my arms and shook me. "You can't do anything!"

Fear rose inside me, threatening to choke off the air I needed to breathe. Sean grabbed my hand and started pulling me away from the barn again. People barreled into us, almost knocking us down, but Sean kept steering me free of the chaos. Everything around me became an orange-tinged blur as he headed for the edge of the clearing surrounding the barn, back toward the wooded area we'd just left. But a fire department pumper truck bounced into the clearing, cutting off our escape route.

Sean stopped, still grasping my hand tightly, and looked for another way out. When he started running again, it was through the edge of the forest, back toward the overgrown entry road. Pine limbs smacked me, twigs and rocks dug into my bare feet, and I twisted my ankle on a fallen limb. I gritted my teeth against the pain shooting up my leg as I tried desperately to keep up with Sean.

I scanned faces as we passed them, but I didn't see Mala or Daniel. I spotted Chad jumping into his car and driving through the bushy areas adjacent to the roadway to get away. Even if everyone got out safely, Mala and I would be grounded for the rest of our lives.

How could I have done this to my grandparents? What if I'd caused them to lose their granddaughter as well as their son?

Amidst the confusion, we bumped into Tommy, who evidently hadn't left after all and was even drunker than when we'd seen him earlier in the evening.

"Where's Mala?" I asked, gasping for air.

"Don't know." His words came out slurred, and he reeked of beer. I was fairly sure he was wearing some of it.

I dug my fingers into his shoulders and shook him. "What happened?"

"We don't have time for this now," Sean said beside me.

"You there, stop," came an adult male voice from several feet behind us.

A frantic glance around us showed that not only had what seemed like the entire sheriff's department shown up, but the way to the vehicles was now blocked by cops stationed there.

Tommy resisted at first, but Sean shook him hard and got right in his face. "Do you want to get arrested?" After all the animosity between them, Sean could have easily turned his back on Tommy. That he didn't showed what a good person he was. Not that I didn't already know that.

Some semblance of common sense overrode Tommy's drunken state, and he allowed Sean and me to drag him away from the craziness. We ran in blind panic to our right, into the thicker darkness that had us tripping over limbs, stumps, rocks, each other. Maneuvering Tommy was like dragging a one-hundred-and-seventy-pound bag of potatoes.

We were running so hard that we nearly toppled into the river when we reached it.

A quick glance over my shoulder showed only dark woods with a hint of firelight. No one else came crashing after us. Rain began to fall as the three of us stood sucking air down into our overworked lungs.

Sean ran his hand through his hair and cursed as he stared at the river cutting off further escape. "What the hell do we do now?"

My brain spun, trying to find an answer to our dilemma. That's when I noticed a splash of light color on the other side of the river. "A raft," I said as I pointed.

Sean stared at the churning water between us and it. He started to take off his shoes to swim across, but I grabbed his arm to stop him.

"There's got to be one on this side somewhere close." We kept emergency rafts tied up at intervals all along the stretch of river we ran, there in case others were damaged or capsized, or as a quick means of escape if there were ever wildfires in the area, like there had been when I was little.

Sean shoved Tommy down on the riverbank. "Don't move," he said through gritted teeth.

I searched in one direction, Sean in the other. My stomach knotted more the longer we scoured the riverbank.

Come on, come on! It's got to be here somewhere.

I let out a cry of relief when I spotted one of the familiar yellow rafts in the bushes a few feet up from the river. My hands shook as I unknotted the ropes, the task made more difficult by the increased amount of rain falling. Once the raft was free, I dragged it down the bank.

"Sean!"

He turned where he was still searching, and I pointed toward the raft. It only took him a few seconds to grab Tommy and steer him toward me. He left Tommy teetering on his feet as he helped me shove the raft into the edge of the water. That's when I realized I couldn't do this. An even more pressing fear wrapped itself around me and squeezed. Yes, I'd been easing my way back into the water with tentative swimming, but that had been in calm and relatively shallow water. Rafting was a different story. Rafting in the dark and rain, down a stretch of river with strong rapids? It was a living, breathing nightmare.

Sean grasped my upper arms and spun me to face him. "Do you want to do this or go back?"

I stared into the forest, back toward the dim glow of the fire. My grandparents would be heartbroken if I were arrested. And what damage would it do to my mother's recovery? A crashing sound in the trees made me jump.

"Let's go," I said.

Sean basically tripped Tommy so that he fell into the raft. Then he and I jumped in and grabbed paddles.

Alongside the consuming terror that made my body go numb and my heart beat wildly, the memory of how to do this resurfaced. Nearly a year had passed since I'd been in a raft, but that time away hadn't erased all the years I'd run this river. My body knew what to do, but my mind was screaming at me to get out, get out now!

The fear crept up my throat like some sort of evil specter, and only grew worse as the rain started falling even harder, making navigating the river more difficult.

In the dark, we slammed into a boulder. I couldn't help the scream that ripped from my throat as I jerked sideways, but the sound was almost immediately swallowed by the sound of the waves and rain.

"You okay?" Sean asked as he looked back at me, his face hard to see in the dark.

I hoped he could see my quick nod, because I couldn't manage anything more. I feared I'd crush the paddle I held with my death grip, but it was the one thing over which I had control. My arms burned with the strain of trying to keep the raft facing forward and not tipping.

God, I wished I could see the river more clearly. I needed to know where we were instead of steering blind.

"Hang on!" Sean yelled.

I braced as we hit a rapid and water sprayed over the side of the raft. The rain beat down harder, pelting us, making our flight so much harder.

The raft jerked again, whipping my neck. I winced but kept staring forward. The rapids eased for a moment, long enough for me to wipe the wet hair out of my eyes just before the current sped up again. Something out of the corner of my eye drew my attention, and when I glanced to the side my heart froze in my chest.

"Oh God, no," I whispered, but the wind and rush of the water drowned out my voice. I knew where we were now. The current hurtled us down the dangerous fork in the river that led through the side canyon where Dad had died. And it was too late to correct the mistake.

Hope drained out of me as flashbacks to my nightmares about drowning slammed into me. But then survival instinct kicked in, and I fought harder with the paddle. I caught glimpses of the slick rock walls of the canyon as we raced by them and imagined how difficult it would be to pull oneself from the river here. How my dad must have died trying.

Even when we floated into a deceptively calm stretch of the river, I couldn't relax. My muscles felt like they'd been ripped to shreds, and they were about to be forced to fight again. I knew that more rapids lay ahead, even worse than the ones we'd just traversed.

"So you all have a good time on your 'walk' through the forest?" Tommy shouted, insinuating he knew exactly what we'd been doing earlier. He looked at Sean and laughed, then tried to give him a high five. "Ah, come on, man. You win."

I didn't like how those words made me feel, like I was some sort of prize in a bet.

"Shut the hell up," Sean said through gritted teeth as he maneuvered us around a boulder.

"Don't get your knickers in such a wad," Tommy said. "Everyone knows you were just trying to one-up me by banging the boss first."

I hated seeing this side of Tommy, someone I normally liked and considered a friend. I glanced at Sean, and despised myself for letting Tommy's words plant doubts in my head. Sean wasn't like that. It was the beer talking.

Even though I knew that—didn't I?—I found it more difficult to steer the raft. Tears welled in my eyes at even the possibility that what we'd shared had been a bet. I shook my head, trying to clear the horrible thoughts. It wasn't true, it wasn't.

"These American girls are such teases," Tommy continued, begging for a pummeling. "Glad you're the one who took her for a ride instead of me."

Sean spun and drew back to punch Tommy, but at that moment, Tommy made an insane attempt to stand up. My scream cut through the sound of the river and rain as Tommy slipped and fell overboard. I saw the horror on Sean's face as he dived to the edge of the raft and grabbed for Tommy's hand to keep him from being swept away. All the motion caused the raft to tip.

Overwhelming dread sliced through me as I felt the raft going over and saw the dark, churning water rising up to capture me. Dear God, my nightmare was coming true.

I heard Sean yell my name as I sank below the waves. Then everything was death-filled water and horrible blackness.

The river had a life of its own, and it was trying to steal mine. It pushed in from all sides, determined to win. My recurring nightmare flashed through my mind, and I flailed against inevitability.

No! It wasn't inevitable. Despite the panic that consumed me, I fought, harder than I ever had, and my head finally broke through the surface of the water. I sucked in precious air while I struggled to reach the edge of the river. Panic bloomed anew a couple of times as I slipped under, but each time I fought my way back to the surface and closer to safety.

After what seemed like many lifetimes, the palms of my hands slapped against the wet rock lining the river. Desperate to be out of the water, I ran one hand along the rock until I found a flat ledge. I felt as if I weighed ten times my normal weight as I pulled myself onto the ledge.

For a split second, I noticed that there were lots of ledges along the river here, places where someone could pull himself to safety. But before I could think about what that meant, my lungs convulsed and I heaved up the murky water I'd swallowed. It came out my mouth and nose and felt like it was destroying my lungs in the process.

Through the tears and rain streaming down my face, I watched the raft hurtle away into the darkness. Despite my continued coughing, I yelled, "Sean! Tommy!" I couldn't stand the thought that they might have drowned. "Sean!"

Sean's and my night together played over the top of my hoarse pleas, my desperation. Please, no, not when I'd just gotten him back again.

The roar of the river and storm swallowed my screams like a black hole, and I couldn't see anything but white-capped water and deep darkness. I was about to totally lose it when I noticed something different coming toward me down the river. On instinct, I stuck out my arm over the water as far as I could and yelled, "Grab my hand!" as loudly as my raw throat would let me.

When someone's hand grasped mine, fighting to keep hold, my eyes widened. It was Sean. A cry of gratitude escaped me. "Hold on, Sean! *Please* hold on!"

We were both totally exhausted from our battle with the river, but through our combined efforts we managed to get him out of the water and onto the ledge. My lungs protested again, and a new wave of coughing wracked my body, accompanied by dizziness. Had I banged my head on a rock?

Past his own retching and coughing, Sean asked, "Where's Tommy?" His voice sounded like someone had sandpapered his vocal cords.

"I don't know," I gasped as a fresh wave of dizziness hit me. The sides of my vision disappeared, creating a scary, black-draped tunnel in front of my eyes, even darker than the night surrounding us. My body started shaking and forced me to lie on my side or risk falling in the river again. My eyes rolled back in my head and everything went totally black.

CHAPTER 23

I woke with my nose twitching. Something smelled funny, like someone had gone crazy with cleaning supplies. I lay still for several moments before I got up the energy to open my eyes. It took a few seconds more to focus against the searing light. Wasn't it supposed to be dark?

Darkness. Rain. Screaming. I sucked in a painful breath, causing Mala to look up from the magazine she was reading in the chair next to my hospital bed. She leaned toward me.

"You're awake." Her words rushed out in relief. I could tell from her red-rimmed eyes that she'd been crying.

"What happened?" I asked, my throat feeling like someone had scrubbed it with a scouring pad. Some parts of my memory were frighteningly clear, others hazy.

"Rescuers checked the river early this morning and found you unconscious on a rock ledge."

A surge of fear slammed into me along with memories of last night. "Sean?"

"He's fine. He was there too, wrapped around you to keep you warm."

I breathed a sigh of relief, but it was short-lived as I noticed the look on Mala's face.

"What's wrong?"

A long moment passed before she raised her eyes. "It's Tommy."

No, my mind screamed. He'd been an ass, yes, but he didn't deserve to drown half a world away from home.

"He's alive, but he's bad. He got banged around on the rocks a lot, and he swallowed a lot of water. He got caught on a fallen tree at the edge of the river. It's the only thing that kept his head above water." Her voice broke, and she bit her quivering bottom lip. "He might not make it."

I turned my head away and stared at the wall, forcing my mind to focus on anything but Tommy's condition.

"How did the fire start?"

Mala sniffed and pulled a tissue from the box on my bedside table. "They said it was someone's cigarette. It lit the hay, and . . . and it went up so fast. I've never been so scared in my life. Daniel and I were in the loft. When we got to the lower level, it was already so smoky." She paused and wrung her hands. "I can't explain it, but I refused to let Daniel lead me out until we checked the rest of the barn. Letting someone burn to death—it was just too awful to think about. When parts of the roof started falling in, Daniel dragged me toward the door. I didn't think we were going to get out."

My head swam at the idea that someone might not have escaped the blaze. "Did anyone else get hurt?"

"Nothing big. Bumps, bruises, a sprained ankle."

Tears stung my eyes as relief and guilt battled it out inside me like a couple of emotional gladiators.

"We shouldn't have taken the river. We should have just gone back and faced the consequences."

Mala placed her hand on my arm, but I wasn't in the mood to be comforted.

"Don't blame yourself," she said. "They didn't have to go. You might have been arrested like Daniel and me. Lots of people got away through the woods or made it to their cars in time, but we didn't."

At least they weren't fighting for their lives.

I half listened as she told me about the aftermath, about how her parents were home now and that she was grounded for the rest of the year.

"Your mom is here too."

That piece of information shocked me out of my daze. I turned my head toward her too quickly, and had to close my eyes while the dizziness ebbed. "Mom's here?" Part of me wanted her to come hold me in her arms and tell me everything would be okay, but I didn't know if Mom had that capacity anymore. My heart weighed heavy in my chest. I didn't want to add to her sorrows, but I couldn't do anything about that now. The deed was done.

"Yeah, she just went to the cafeteria. Grandma made her."

"How long have I been here?"

"Since early this morning."

By glancing at the window, I could tell it was now nearly night again.

"Is Sean here somewhere?"

"He was discharged. His parents took him home."

"Which home?"

"His dad's. He was pretty torn up about you, and Tommy. I've never seen him look like that. His parents had to force him to leave."

The scene of Sean drawing back to hit Tommy and then Tommy falling overboard played again in my mind, clearer this time. "Why did he do it?"

"What?"

I took a deep breath that hurt my lungs; then I told her about what had happened in the minutes prior to our capsizing. Mala looked down at her lap and started wringing her hands again.

"What is it?"

"Tommy didn't leave the party. Chad saw him outside. Tommy . . . watched you and Sean walk off toward the woods together."

A horrible thought occurred to me. "He didn't follow us, did he?"

"No. He came back inside and got roaring drunk. When he wakes up, I plan to get him a year's supply of Starbucks and tell him to drink that instead. Hyper Tommy is better than drunk Tommy."

I was surprised to feel myself smile, but the grin faded almost as quickly as it appeared. The guilt inside me was too strong and demanding. First Dad, now Tommy. Why hadn't I *insisted* that my family sell the business and leave here sooner? Before something else bad happened?

Because, once again, I'd wanted desperately to be with Sean. I had pushed all other concerns aside and let him occupy all my thoughts. Had being with him again cost someone else his life?

But I knew for sure this time it wasn't his fault.

It was mine.

CHAPTER 24

I felt detached when I was released from the hospital a day after being brought in. The same kind of numbness that had shrouded me after word of Dad's death found its way back to me. It made me move slower than normal as I walked the few steps from the wheelchair outside the hospital doors to Mom's car. Everyone around me murmured encouragement, thinking my sluggish movements were because of the physical trauma I'd been through, my cut feet and battered body. But it was as if I were trying to walk through a fog the thickness of cold maple syrup.

"Here you go, sweetie," Mom said as she helped me lift my legs into the car. "We'll be home soon and you can rest."

When my scrapes and bruises healed, I knew I'd receive my punishment for the party fiasco. But for now, Mom only seemed concerned with my welfare—which made me feel horrible and want to demand my punishment now. I deserved it, after all. Tommy lay in the hospital, still unconscious. I'd gone by to see him before leaving and had found his aunt in the room on the phone to his parents en route from London. From the sound of the conversation, this hadn't been the first time Tommy had found himself in a bad spot because of drinking. Still, I prayed for the Tommy I knew without the alcohol and left the doorway before his aunt turned around and saw me. Even if he hated me when he woke up, I wanted him to wake up—and soon.

Mala's parents had allowed her to stay behind at the hospital to help Tommy's family any way she could. I prayed she'd call me later to say Tommy had woken up, that he was on the road to recovery.

When Mom slipped into the driver's seat of the car, I looked at her profile. For the first time, I realized she'd gotten a haircut, a shorter, angled-at-the-chin style that made her look younger than her forty-one years. I watched her face, expecting her to crack at any moment. My heart ached at what I'd done to her, too. She'd nearly lost her only child to the same river that had claimed her husband only a year before. If I sent her into deep depression again, I'd never forgive myself.

But the only signs she gave of being agitated were a tenseness along her jaw and the way she gripped and released the steering wheel over and over.

I turned my head and stared out the window without really seeing. I felt alone and adrift. The warmth of Mom's hand on mine shocked me. She squeezed it in a show of support and comfort I didn't deserve.

"I'm sorry I wasn't here when you needed me," she whispered, staring ahead at the road.

I didn't know why, but those simple words were what finally cracked the shell around me. Tears spilled down my cheeks. "It's all my fault," I said, the words ripping at my sore throat.

She gripped my hand tighter. "No, don't. You didn't start that fire."

"But it wouldn't have happened if we hadn't had the party, if we hadn't run, if I hadn't been so selfish." Each word hurt more than the last, but the pain was fitting. I should have had to scream until my throat bled.

"We all make mistakes," Mom said, trying to calm me.

I jerked my head around and stared at her through my tears. "Why are you doing that?"

"What?"

"Trying to make me feel better?" My voice broke. "I don't deserve that. My selfishness keeps leading to tragedy, and you want to make me feel *better* about it."

"Honey, what are you talking about?" She glanced at me like I'd lost my grip on reality. Maybe I had. And maybe that was a good thing. Reality hurt too much.

"Tommy. Dad." My heart squeezed, and I took a shaky breath. "Neither of them would have gotten hurt if I hadn't been so determined to be with Sean."

"Your dad?" Mom sounded surprised and looked at me with questions in her eyes. "Alex, you had nothing to do with that."

"Didn't I?" I asked, my voice raised, banging off the confines of the car. "I should have gone down the river with him that day instead of going off with Sean, shouldn't have let him raft alone when he was feeling so bad. I should have been able to help him forget Iraq and remember how good his life here was. But I didn't! I failed him, and he's dead! Dead!" I slammed my fist against the car's console. "Now I've maybe killed Tommy, too."

Mom swerved off the road into the parking lot of an abandoned building, switched off the car's ignition, and took a deep, halting breath of her own before turning toward me. She grasped my hands in hers, and when I tried to pull away she tightened her grip and shook me.

"Your father's death was *not* your fault. How could you think that?"

I looked down, ashamed to meet my mother's eyes. "Grandma told you what happened to him in Iraq. If I'd tried harder to make him forget Sanaa and how she died, to make him happy again, he wouldn't have been so distracted. He would have paid attention to where he was and not gone down the wrong branch of the river." More tears poured out of my eyes, accompanied by sobs that hurt my battered lungs.

"Alex, sweetheart, sometimes people just can't be saved," Mom said, her voice breaking and tears pooling in her eyes. "They're so broken they give up."

I shook my head, ignoring the way it made my eyes cross and temples throb. "That's a lie." My dad was strong, always had been. He wouldn't give up. He'd fight to live. "Why do people keep saying things like that?"

She squeezed my hands again. "Because it's true," she said, her voice a raspy whisper full of sadness, but also acceptance. "Sometimes people go through such terrible things that they lose the will to live, and no one can force that desire back into them." She reached up and pushed the hair out of my face and back over my shoulder. "Not even daughters who love their fathers."

I pulled away, and this time she let me. I stared out the window, and something I'd never thought possible happened. My heart broke even more. She and Mala were right.

Dad hadn't tried to live. If he'd tried to, he would have. If I'd been able to pull myself from the river at night in a rainstorm, he could have done it during a clear day.

He hadn't wanted to.

Fresh tears trekked down my cheeks. I felt like I was losing him all over again. All the anguish of the past year, much of which I'd kept from my fragile mother, came pouring out. Mom pulled me into her arms, and I soaked the front of her blouse in a matter of seconds. She stroked my hair and whispered a soothing "shh" in my ear.

"You have to let it go. What happened to your dad was tragic, but it had nothing to do with you. And Tommy is responsible for his own actions." She kissed my forehead and hugged me tighter. "It's time we move on with our lives."

I tried to push away, but Mom wouldn't let me. "But I'm a horrible, selfish person!"

Mom pulled back from me and looked into my eyes. "No, you're not. Don't ever say that. You were so strong for me, even when it was I who should have been strong for you. And you've helped your grandparents run the business when you could have been out having fun with your friends."

She lifted her hand to push my loose hair back from my face. "Wanting to be with someone you love isn't selfish."

Mom wiped away some of my tears. "I love you, Alex. Lots of people do. Don't let what happened make you push us away. We need you as much as you need us."

I thought it would take me a long time to go to sleep that night, but my exhausted body had other ideas. So when my cell phone rang early the next morning, I had to drag myself out of the fog of sleep to answer it. I didn't even open my eyes to see whose name was on the display.

"Hello?"

A moment passed before Sean said, "Hey."

My eyes popped open. "What's wrong?" I knew him well enough to interpret the sound of his voice.

He took a shaky breath, and I knew before he said the words.

"Tommy died early this morning."

The black pit yawned below me again, and it took all my effort not to fall in. "God, no," I whispered.

"His parents . . . his parents barely got here in time." I'd never heard Sean's voice sound so strained, not even when Dad had died and I'd blamed him.

I pulled myself to a sitting position on the side of my bed and wiped away new tears. Tommy, gone. I couldn't wrap my mind around it, couldn't really believe it. He'd been so incredibly full of life. How could someone like that be dead?

"Are you there?" I asked, about to choke on the lump in my throat.

"I was earlier."

"Where are you now?"

"Just walking."

I thought I heard the river in the background, and I tried not to let my nerves shift into overdrive. Sean wouldn't do anything stupid, and fate wouldn't be so cruel as to rip someone else from my life. I had to believe that, had to let Sean deal with Tommy's death however he needed to, even though I wanted to run to him and wrap him in my arms.

"Listen, I'll call you later," Sean said, then hung up before I could respond.

I held the phone to my ear for several seconds before flipping it closed and pressing it against my chest. Mom had said someday the pain would fade. I wanted that day to be today.

The next couple of weeks passed by in a haze. Each day, the black ribbon on the front door of the office reminded me of Tommy. Though we were in the middle of our busy season, our family decided not to hire another river guide. We just booked fewer trips. It didn't feel right to even think about replacing Tommy as if he were an air conditioner gone bad. I helped with everything except the actual guiding down the river. I'd faced that monster once, but I wasn't sure I'd be able to do it a second time.

Each day was a carbon copy of the one before, with only the faces of the customers changing. We all went through the motions of running the business, and Mala and I spent each afternoon helping to rebuild the barn. Neither of us complained. We deserved this punishment and much more.

One afternoon while waiting to drive to the takeout point to pick up the day's last rafters, I parked myself on the top step on the back porch and watched the river flow by. My feelings about it were mixed, the same as my feelings about what the future held. Did I want to go ahead with the plan to leave, maybe go to Denver, where Sean and I could still see each other? Or did I stay and fight my way back to a truce with the river?

"Maybe you were right," Mala said as she sank down beside me and propped her arms on her knees.

"About?"

"Leaving before something else bad happened."

Dozens of good times on the river flashed through my mind. Cookouts at the beach. Good-natured teasing between those of us guiding different rafts down the river. My dad's bad attempts at singing campfire songs that echoed through the canyons during overnight excursions. Me and Sean stealing kisses when we were supposed to be collecting firewood to keep our guests warm on cool Colorado nights.

My dad talking about how much he loved the river, how it was as much a part of him as his blood.

"I don't know what the right thing to do is," I said.

Everything seemed so up in the air, even Sean's and my relationship. I felt awful for thinking about it in the face of Tommy's death, but I couldn't help it. We spent time together at work, and Sean helped with the barn rebuilding, as did Daniel and Chad, but no words had been spoken about what we'd shared before the fire. It was like his mind was somewhere else.

One day nearly two weeks after Tommy's death, Sean didn't show up for work. When Mom caught me looking for him, she said, "He went to visit his mom for a few days."

"Oh." He'd gone without telling me. I tried to push down the feelings of doubt Tommy's words in the raft had created deep within me.

I managed to slog through the rest of the workday before I gave in and texted Sean. When I didn't receive a response, I told myself he was busy or his phone was turned off. He'd get back in touch with me when he was able. Or maybe he was doing the guy thing and keeping to himself while he dealt with his guilt over Tommy's death. Why had I let him go without telling him that it wasn't his fault? Especially when I knew how that type of guilt chewed a person up inside.

When I reached my bedroom, Tommy's accusatory words replayed over and over in my head. I couldn't make them stop. I started punching my pillow, only a few times at first. But then the punches came harder and faster, until my pillow could have sued me for assault and battery. I finally sank onto the foot of my bed and hugged the pillow to me, wishing instead it were Sean.

Why hadn't I told him that I loved him?

CHAPTER 25

August waned with the flurry of late-summer rafters trying to get in a few more trips downriver before the kids had to go back to school. Work continued on autopilot for all of us as Labor Day weekend approached. For the second year in a row, we were in mourning.

"I suppose we can schedule a couple more trips on Labor Day," Mom said from the office's front counter. What she didn't say was that we normally closed early that day so we could enjoy our annual family and employee cookout. Last year had been the first time in my life we'd not gone all out on Labor Day and eaten ourselves silly. Maybe we'd never have those events again.

"I think we should have the cookout," Mala said, surprising me, Mom, and Grandma, who was cleaning out the office fridge. "I mean, what if we had it in remembrance of Tommy and Uncle Steve? They did both love a good party." Mala scanned all of our faces with a "Did I just say the wrong thing?" expression on hers.

The quiet stretched for an uncomfortable length of time, and I worried as I always did that something would break

Mom again. But she'd been surprising me lately with her renewed strength. She did so again now when she looked up from the schedule and said, "I think that's a good idea. We could all use a little fun. We should remember the good times and try to get past the bad."

I caught Mom's gaze, and she gave me a little smile. I'd never been prouder of her. She had walked through the darkness of depression and despair and come out the other side.

Laughter seemed tentative at the cookout in Grandma and Grandpa's backyard, but everyone also seemed glad to have normalcy slowly creeping back into their lives.

I watched through the open kitchen window as Chad stepped up in front of Mom, holding his plate out for another burger.

Mom smiled and shook her head. "Child, I swear you could eat an entire cow if we put it in front of you."

"Let the boy eat, Emily," Grandpa said. "He'll be tackling those players from Parson in another week."

I smiled at the exchange, then scanned the rest of the people spread across the lawn.

Mala and Daniel walked hand in hand through the crowd. She had repaired her relationship with her parents after a long, heartfelt conversation. And they'd been thrilled when they found out she and Daniel were officially a couple. I suspected they were relieved because Daniel wasn't a guy who'd cause them worry when he was with Mala. They were also proud of how she'd stepped in to help Tommy's family in the days before they'd left to fly his body home to England.

Despite Cooley Mountain Whitewater's latest loss, I hadn't broached the topic of possibly selling the rafting business with my family. I honestly didn't know how I felt about it anymore. I kept putting off the conversation and finally decided not to even consider saying anything until we closed for the year in a couple of weeks. We only had weekend trips after today anyway, since school started in two days.

I retrieved another bowl of Grandma's potato salad from the refrigerator and headed outside with it. As I stepped through the doorway, I nearly ran into Sean. The bowl slipped from my hands, but Sean caught it.

"Some reflexes, huh?"

I didn't answer, simply stared at him.

"You okay?" he asked, concern etching his brow.

I managed a nod. "It's just good to see you." Even though he'd only been gone a few days, I'd battled the fear that he'd left for good this time.

"You too." He stared at me for a moment, then lifted the bowl. "Where does this go?"

I took the bowl back and headed toward the nearest table of food.

He fell into step beside me. "Looks good."

"Seems to be popular. This is the third bowl." We were still in superficial conversation land as far as our relationship went, but I sensed he wanted to say something.

"Can you go for a walk?"

I glanced at Mom. I was grounded, after all. She gave me one of those "Mom knows everything" looks and nodded.

We started walking slowly toward the stand of pines lining the ridge above the river. Sean wrapped his hand around mine, and it felt so good to be touching him again that I didn't say anything for fear he'd take his hand away. Instead, I let memories of our last time in the woods wash over me.

"I'm sorry I haven't said anything about that night," he said. "I know I should have, but my head got all messed up." He waved his hand at his head as if implying he was halfway crazy. "All I was able to think about was how guilty I felt about Tommy, about being mad at him for insulting you and how if I hadn't started to hit him he might still be alive."

I placed my hand on his upper arm. "Don't. It wasn't your fault. He started to stand before you ever made a move. He was just drunk and not thinking clearly. I'm not even really sure he realized he was in a raft."

He turned to face me. "I want you to know the things he said weren't true. I wasn't trying to one-up him by having sex with you."

"I know. He was just jealous—and hurt." I'd come to that realization in the days after Mom and I had talked. I hadn't mentioned the sex thing to her, and she hadn't asked, but she'd been certain Sean loved me. She didn't even freak out that her sixteen-year-old daughter was talking about being in love. No speeches about how I was too young to know what being in love really meant. It made me wonder how long she'd loved Dad before he'd gotten a clue and asked her out.

Sean pulled something from his pocket and held it in his outstretched palm. I recognized the old blue handkerchief that had hidden his secret item from the time capsule. "Take it."

My curiosity flared, and I took the bundle before he changed his mind. I unwrapped it, and inside was a clear plastic container like the kind from gum-ball machines. Inside that was a cheap ring made to look like a square sapphire surrounded by diamonds.

"Do you remember that?"

A vague memory of the machine in the lobby of the IGA grocery store, one of those that had metal grabbers used for attempting to snatch prizes, floated to the front of my mind. I swallowed against the lump forming in my throat.

"You really liked that ring," he said. "It took several dollars, but I finally got it. But then I was too chicken to give it to you."

"Why?"

"Um, because I was in fifth grade. And we were buddies. Giving you a ring didn't feel like a buddy thing to do." He shrugged. "So I put it in the time capsule thinking I'd give it to you when we were older and I had more guts."

Mom had been right.

Sean lifted his hand to my cheek and skimmed the pad of his thumb over my skin. I closed my eyes to drink in the sensation. My heart had been through a lot during the past year, times when I thought it would shatter from the pain. But now the tremendous happiness I was feeling was healing all those broken places.

"I love you, Alex. I think I always have." He leaned down and kissed me with what really did feel like true love.

Time would tell, I guessed.

After we kissed for several minutes, we sat on a log in silence for a long time, just soaking up being with each other. It was simple, but that was the beauty of it.

When the sun dipped to a point where it was shining in at an angle through the trees, Sean shifted against me. "We should head back before your mom sends a search party."

He helped me to my feet, and we walked with our hands linked back toward the party. I glanced toward a bird gliding on the air thermals high above the river and spotted the old rafting ropes hanging from one of the trees stretching over the edge of the cliff. I pointed to them.

"Remember how we all used to swing out on those and jump into the river?"

"Yeah."

I slipped my hand out of his and walked over to the tree, grabbed one of the ropes and tested its strength. Still solid and sturdy. I glanced back at Sean. "You know, I've loved you ever since then."

Realization struck him, then understanding.

As Mala once said, we only live once and we should go after what we want. Now that I had Sean, I desperately wanted to recapture my love of the river, a deep love I'd shared with my dad, the rest of my family, and all my closest friends.

Just as it had been for Dad, this river was as much a part of me as the molecules that made up my body. And I wasn't about to leave my molecules behind.

I walked backward with the rope in my hands. I inhaled a deep, slow breath, then ran as fast as I could toward the edge of the cliff. I swung out over the river and instinct took over.

As I let go of the rope, a familiar shot of pure joy surged through me at being part of this river, of this wild place.

Acknowledgments

Heartbreak River never would have seen publication if fellow author and wonderful friend Stephanie Rowe hadn't encouraged me to write young adult novels. Thanks, Steph! Thanks also to my agent, Michelle Grajkowski, for being a champion for my stories, and to editor extraordinaire Lexa Hillyer for believing in me and Heartbreak River. There aren't words to express what you all and this opportunity means to me.

A very special thanks to my husband, Shane, who has been my hero and unflagging supporter for half of my life.